1

My name's Colin Todd and I'm a private investigator. I know, a name as exciting as beige wallpaper. You couldn't imagine a movie called the Colin Ultimatum or Liam Neeson whispering down the phone, 'I'm Colin, and I want my family back.' It did make for a great bedfellow in alliteration when a kid though, 'clumsy Colin' was popular. Another c-word got added at uni, but I'll leave you to imagine what that was. To spice things up a bit, I once had the brilliant idea of changing my name to Mr Jarse, first name Hugh, but thought better of it in the end.

How did a Colin become a PI? Good question; I'm not sure myself. It wasn't a career I chose; it chose me by circumstance. I spent my university days drinking and trying (sometimes successfully) to have sex. That lifestyle choice was prevalent for the 1st and 2nd years. None of us knew what we wanted to do as a career unless they were studying one of the professions or computer science. The careers adviser was as useful as a chocolate teapot in that regard.

"What's the best way to get a job after leaving college?" I asked at the only pointless session we ever had. I had to attend, it was a university requirement for anyone doing a degree there. All students pretty much never went, and the so-called adviser couldn't give a fig if anyone came or not. He was still paid and had zero interest in how we benefited from this gift of higher education. We could have been homeless for all he cared.

"Give up that degree and become an undertaker. Trust me, you'll work less hours, always have a demand for your services and be a lot richer. You can even be a really terrible undertaker and still do well; the dead don't complain," was his sage advice.

The 3rd year came as a massive shock to us all. In football parlance, it was the business end of the championship with final exams and a dissertation. Everything we should've learned in the preceding years was supposed to provide the bedrock for completing the third year. The problem was that no one paid any attention in those first two years, so we suddenly had to catch up on the work. The partying was temporarily put on hold. I was studying politics and economics, the politics bit was easier to catch up with than the economics bit. I just scraped a 2:1and was half a per cent off a Desmond (Tutu). Armed with this higher education certificate (which no one ever asked to see post-uni), I felt the world was ready for my talents. I just wasn't sure what they were or where a good fit sat. So I temped.

There were quite a few office filing jobs, working with girls who would go out at lunchtime, drink gin with slimline tonic and eat baked potatoes because they were watching their weight. Their efforts to slim never worked because it wasn't the tonic water or even the gin making them fat. All the chocolate, cakes, crisps, KFCs, burgers and curries they shoved down their large gobs saw off the skinny beings within them. It wasn't just office work, I did get out and about. Cleaning out the fat from the sewers was a particular highlight. A long broom handle with a hook on the end was used to break up all the congealed fat that had made its way down to the sewers from London's kitchen sinks. That may not sound too bad, but the solidified fat acted like a sieve, catching every unimaginable object from toilets across the capital. Coming back smelling of sewers on the tube, people moved down the carriage away from me holding their noses. I threw up violently the first time and only did one more day before realising it just wasn't worth it. There was a week assisting the chief inseminator at a battery turkey farm. This involved handing him a clean syringe after each large bird had been given its dose. I also made up survey answers, pretended to make cold sales calls and filled in for a 'waste operative' or binman to you and me.

At least it was money coming in, allowing me to move into a

shared flat. The ad said, 'Cabin crew looking for flatmate in lovely, modern apartment. I'm always away so it will be like your own place a lot of the time.' This sounded perfect. I imagined having the apartment to myself whilst they travelled, and then when they were back, I would meet all her crew friends. I thought I'd have a whale of a time. My heart sank when I rang the buzzer, and Gerald opened the door. Like that riddle where someone assumes the surgeon is male, I thought cabin crew meant hot female. I still took the room though as it was a really lovely flat. Gerald and I ended up terrific friends and of course, he did have plenty of crew friends, including hot female ones, I was introduced to. It was an utter blast.

On my way back after a heavy afternoon where my job was to check tickets at a venue where a particular teen heartthrob boy band was playing, I was in shock. As any parent of a teenage girl knows, when they get together and scream (even a couple of them), the result is a sound used by dictators worldwide as torture. I kept checking my ears to see if they were bleeding because they felt like they'd blown up by explosives. Then, whilst working out if I had gone deaf, I saw an ad for the Metropolitan Police. They had a graduate scheme and were recruiting ex-students with the necessary skill set. Anything was better than traipsing around from job to job each day.

I was surprised by the application form. A question asked if the applicant had any criminal convictions. I thought that surely if they did, they were a) applying for the wrong career and b) would get rejected straight away. But no, on reading the accompanying explanatory notes, a criminal conviction didn't necessarily rule out the applicant. I should have seen this 'all inclusive' wokery pokery as a warning sign. In my book, if you have a criminal conviction, that rules you out of a career where your job is to make sure a criminal is caught and gets a conviction. This was the reason I left in the end. Hindsight's a wonderful thing.

I joined the scheme as a trainee detective constable. I thought this would have a detrimental effect on my friendships. Most of them liked a bit of puff, occasionally mind-bending hallucinogens and the odd bit of Charlie. My university friends hadn't followed me to London at that time. They were still working in pubs in their home cities, towns or villages while applying for work. Some did this with more gusto than others. They'd grown used to the hotel of Mum and Dad. They were reluctant to move into digs that should have been condemned just to escape from the folks and the accompanying daily maid and meal service they provided. So I never saw them, we just exchanged hilarious messages in the group using 70's references from The Sweeney like 'I'll kick your arse to your shoulder blades' and a lot of 'Shut It!' and 'Get your trousers on, you're nicked'. The humour masked a slight worry amongst them about letting on about the sort of drug behaviour or illegal raves they were up to.

Gerald and the gang found the whole thing hilarious. They only altered the way they acted around me by asking questions and wanting to know all the gory details of cases of training. They almost had parties just to hear stories like my first dead body. It was a naked fat man who'd had a heart attack whilst masturbating to porn. When we turned up, I had no idea what to expect, but the smell was the first thing to hit me. It was so acrid and rancid that it made me gag and want to throw up immediately. My colleague, a proper DC, had experienced it before and had put a handkerchief to his mouth and nose. I could tell he was smiling underneath, part of the initiation, don't tell the rookie. I didn't actually vomit and the DC lost his bet back at the station on the number of seconds it would take me to expel my stomach contents. The porn was still on repeat on the giant TV. The mound of flesh that used to be a person did not resemble the flesh on the screen in the slightest. It had turned a bluish-purple colour due to blood not being pumped around the body. The whole cadaver had also started to bloat because of the gas build up from decomposing innards. It was all surreal, and there was even a morbid joke or two shared by the DC. The Daliesque feeling lasted until I was given the job of telling his son about his father's demise straight after we left the deceased. That was one of the most horrific experiences of my life and one not to be repeated when we're talking light-heartedly.

I rose to Detective Seargent in 6 years, which actually was quite an achievement. When I qualified as Detective Constable, I had thought that to get promotion, I just had to 'nick people' as Regan would have said. But there were a lot of exams to do, which was unexpected and unwanted. Nevertheless, I managed to do OK in them (you didn't need to be all superstar, a pass would do) and had a few good cases with positive outcomes.

Then came Trevor Smith to change my career path. A particularly militant group of Trans activists, upset about something people couldn't quite make out, had adopted a tactic from environmental protesters. They aimed to mess up and ruin as many people's days as possible to highlight their cause. So they glued themselves gantries on the M25, causing horrific delays of up to six hours on the network. One driver caught up in the chaos was Trevor, who'd been called by the care home his mother was in. She was on the way out and he needed to get there asap to say his goodbyes. But because these guys were making a point about something they were furious about, Trevor never got to say farewell to his mum. So when the group tweeted a photo of their 'heroes' on various gantries, it sent Trevor into a rage. He tweeted them:

What gives you lot pretending to be birds, the right ruin everyone's fucking day

This, of course, caused a Twitter meltdown as other activists worldwide started wading in. The attacks just spurred Trevor on to more prose.

You look like a bunch of fucking blokes in wigs with shit makeup going to a fancy dress party IN YOUR NAN'S FUCKING CLOTHES

He was shouting in type, a clear sign of getting slightly unhinged. The exchanges continued for days and although he garnered support from certain people, a perpetually angry activist group pretending to be a charity got involved. That's when I was instructed to investigate a hate crime committed by Trevor. When I reported back the facts about why he was so angry and there was mitigation for his ranting online, I was told to go and arrest him anyway. That was the day I handed in my resignation. It had nothing to do with the issue. I firmly believed that everyone had the right to live their lives as whoever they wanted to be, just as long as that was not Hitler or Stalin. I would fight for anyone's right to identify as a sheep if that makes them happy. So the issue wasn't the problem. The problem was I just couldn't be bothered with the police anymore. The bureaucracy, paperwork, wokeness and lack of resources were all sources of inner angst. We had seemed to give up on things like burglary or car theft and focus on areas that only affected a minuscule proportion of the country's lives. I was angry that my time, the police's time and then the resources of all the other agencies that would get involved, were deemed so inconsequential. That everything could be used to arrest Trevor, charge and take him to court. Policing wasn't a vocation for me, just something other than the other jobs. Once in the force, I didn't have the gumption to get out until Trevor came along.

2

I thought it was time to ditch public transport. The tube didn't work properly and was unhealthy; there were laws against transporting animals in the sort of temperatures and overcrowding that in the summer. The bus wasn't much of an option either. You had to wait while exposed to all weather conditions and really did only come along in threes. They took an eternity to get anywhere and seemed to have quite an undesirable element amongst their passengers. Every night in the London Evening Standard, there was a story about someone on a bus being stabbed or having some other form of horrible violence exacted upon them. Driving was out because there were never any parking spaces and the congestion charge meant it was too expensive.

So my chosen mode of transport was a scooter or Piaggio Vespa to be more precise. Not the electric death traps that anyone can drive and crash, the motorised petrol ones you sit on and need tax, insurance, MOT and a helmet to ride. With this, I always found a parking space, never queued in traffic and was 15 minutes away from anywhere in London. Just keeping possession of the bike, however, was always a challenge. Every little hoon too young or poor to buy a car always had their eyes open for someone else's moped. I had three stolen over the space of a few months. The other problem was the inherent danger. While not as dangerous as the big bikes, being knocked off one could still cause considerable damage. An anaesthetist friend would describe, in graphic detail, the motorbike injuries she had to deal with. When they came off, the guys going 70 to 100 mph were brought into the operating theatre in bits. Scooter injuries weren't as horrific, but scary enough to make her swear she'd never get on or own one. This danger became nigh on suicidal in the wet because the wheels are so small they have no grip whatsoever in the rain, as I discovered one morning. The bike was going as fast as it could (30 mph) down a long, straight road when a post office van turned in front of me. As recommended by the guy who sold me the bike, I pulled on the brakes, an equal distribution of pressure between front and back wheels. The salesman had neglected to tell me that in those conditions, you might as well jump off for all the use they were. The wheels locked up and the scooter disappeared from underneath me. Now minus a bike, I skidded on my back, feet first, towards the post office van. I could see the vehicle's underside looming ever nearer in slow motion. The bike careered across the road and hit the driver's door of a dustbin lorry. Just as I skidded towards the front of the van, my feet seemed to catch on something in the road, miraculously flipping and depositing me across the front. I was face to face with the driver, separated only by the windscreen and the open-face helmet. My nose and lips squashed against the glass, making a slight screeching sound as I slid down the glass and landed in the road on my back.

"Jesus, you alright, mate?" enquired the worried driver. I was prostrate, looking up at the sky, which was now being filled by his face. I couldn't entirely focus on what had just happened. Was I still alive? Was I hurt? If this was heaven, it was a severe letdown. "Try and get up," the driver offered helpfully. I didn't respond to the encouragement, so he moved closer. "Here, let me give you a hand," he said as he reached out and grabbed my arm. Although still not quite comprehending what had happened, I felt a surge of anger towards the man.

"What! You want to move me? Don't you know you're not supposed to move a motorbike crash victim in case you cause more damage? Jesus, even my 5-year-old nephew knows that," I shouted as I got up.

"All right, mate. I'm only trying to help. " The driver was getting defensive.

"Trying to help. Really? Well, here's how you can help. First, invent a time machine to take you back a few minutes. Then, when you're sitting at the junction about to turn — don't fucking do it. Just stay there."

"There's no need for that. You're obviously OK, so I'm off, " he said, climbing back in the van.

"Oh yeah, better get back quickly or the whole postal system will collapse around us. Don't worry about me. I'll just look for a mangled wreckage that used to be my bike. " I could see him mouthing 'wanker' as he drove away. Only after he'd disappeared did it dawn on me to get his details for insurance purposes. I looked over at the dustbin lorry still sitting at the traffic lights. My bike was on its side in the road, engine still running. I suddenly became aware of a searing pain in my right ankle and couldn't put any pressure on it. My trousers were ripped down from the thigh. The top of my shoe flapped about, exposing a bloody foot through a ripped sock. I hopped over to the lorry and looked up at the three men in the front of the cab, all wearing fluorescent yellow tops. There wasn't a flicker of emotion on their faces as they looked down at me.

"Thanks for your help guys. Very kind of you. " The lights turned green and the lorry moved off. 'Don't suppose you got his number? " I shouted at the driver.

Apart from missing a wing mirror and all the paint off one side, the bike wasn't too severely damaged, so I rode it to the hospital. The nearest one was held up as a shining example of what the NHS could genuinely do. The common areas had galleried walkways, and a fountain in the vast atrium, exotic plants, and modern art were hanging along all the corridors. The A&E, however, was just like any other anywhere in the country. It was busy and populated with a collection of the walking wounded, all looking really sorry for themselves. I half expected to see my anaesthetist friend to come in, point her finger and say, 'I told you so.' Instead, I was starting to shiver a bit with shock.

About an hour later, the door in the corner of the enormous waiting room opened and a stern-looking female medic barked, 'Mr. Todd'. My mind elsewhere, I stood up and started for her. Forgetting why I was there in the first place, I pushed off on my right foot and promptly collapsed into a pile of stacked plastic chairs, knocking them all across the room. No help from anyone, not even the medic, who just looked at me coolly. Once I'd composed myself, I hopped over to her. On closer inspection, she was cute.

"Follow me please," she instructed, walking down to the end cubicle, leaving me behind. From the examination room, she watched me hop for about 20 feet along the corridor.

"Now, Mr Havers, what's the problem?" she asked as we were seated in the cubicle. In hindsight, I definitely shouldn't have said it, but I wasn't in the best of moods. She'd just seen me hop for England and my bleeding foot was exposed through a ripped shoe.

"It's my arm, Doctor," I said in a deadpan way and waited for a smile from her pretty face. There was no reaction at all, just silence and an icy stare. It must have been a bad day for her as well. "I'm sorry, that was a bad joke. It's my ankle."

My attempt at humour really came back to haunt me. I waited four hours for the X-ray results. It seemed like hundreds of people had been admitted after me and all left with their results. Each time the doc walked past me, she asked whoever was sitting nearby if they were being dealt with and apologised for any delay. Each time I tried to talk to her, she just ignored me. Eventually, I was called into the results room and faced my nemesis.

"The cuts to your foot are quite minor and don't need any stitches." It was as if she was giving out to me for wasting her time with such trifling ailments. "You've also torn a ligament in your ankle. There's no treatment for this apart from Paracetamol and keeping it up and rested."

"Oh, how long will it be before I can walk on it? " I inquired.

"Depends, " she said, staring blankly at me.

"On what? "

"Well, some can take a couple of months to heal, others six or nine months.'

"Jesus, that's a long time. "

"It would have been better if you'd broken it.' She was actually enjoying telling me this. 'With a break, you'd have had it in plaster for six weeks and then it would be healed. "

"Can I at least get some crutches? "'

"No, there are people with more serious injuries, you know. People far worse off and they really need them. Crutches don't grow on trees, you know. "

"Well, technically, the wooden…"

"Goodbye, Mr Todd."

That day, I'd been on my way to meet an ex-colleague who'd gone down the PI route. We had to postpone face-to-face, so the dreaded Zoom took its place. He really sold me on how great the investigator's way of earning money was and the joys of being your own boss. If I didn't want to fill in paperwork, I didn't fill in paperwork. I'd have no manager to report to, no one above me that couldn't run a bath, let alone a department. That report about how the department was living up to its inclusivity goals – gone. I'd pay less tax too. There were loads to claim against, such as transport, equipment needed for investigations and even beer as an essential part of my work in getting people to give information unhindered by sobriety. It sounded perfect. He didn't explain that it doesn't matter about paying tax or even trying to pay as little as possible. If you have no clients, you have no earnings or expenses anyway. He also didn't tell me how to market myself with a website, advertising, etc. I got the hang of it (sort of) by trial and error.

3

Although a Private Investigator's licence is not required to be a PI in the UK, I was advised to get one if I wanted higher paying jobs. The main thing was I had to pass a 'fit & proper person test', which involved eligibility checks and an assessment conducted by an external body. It so happened that the person running my checks and interview for the licence had been at the first station when I joined the police. He was a very likeable fellow, we always had gotten on well and realising it was me who the interviewee was, he just said, 'We don't need this now, do we.' So he signed a load of forms and we went for a pint or two.

I didn't blaze a trail of glory early in my new career. The calibre of cases wasn't exactly Columbo. For example, finding the person responsible for training a dog to defecate on his neighbour's doorstep. They'd had an argument about bins which sent the canine owner into a hate-filled rage and a sense of retribution. He had spent months training George, the boxer dog, to do his business in that same spot daily. I set up motion-triggered cameras on his building façade, something he could have done himself. He did the walk at 3am when everyone was asleep and after the act each morning, he gave George a dog biscuit as a reward.

Eventually, the cases got more intricate and better paying. My first adultery job signalled a move into more meaty investigations. Martin Hearst's wife approached me, saying she suspected him of having an affair. I later learned that it was usually true in 99.9% of my cases where one party suspects the other of infidelity. Of course, when first approached about these infidelities, I should have told them those statistics, but then I wouldn't eat. The Hearst job should have been straightforward, but it wasn't for a rookie PI. I made all the mistakes in the book, which culminated in a broken nose. I was stalking the errant hubby as he took his secretary out to dinner. She was at least half his age and possessed specific attributes the unfortunate Mrs Hearst didn't. I thought I was discreetly taking photos through the restaurant window from behind a pillar outside. There was no way the mark could see me doing that. That was the thinking anyway. I hadn't noticed he was sitting under a mirrored ceiling, one in which, when he looked up, he could see me clearly as day, taking photos of him with his blonde dinner date. After 20 minutes, he got up from the table, I guessed to go to the toilet. I had enough evidence, so I decided to call it a day. On rounding the corner of the building heading for my car, I remember it going black and a searing pain in my nose. It was Mr Hearst and he didn't bother asking any questions, just went straight for the punch. I wasn't expecting the aggrieved wife's reaction.

"What the fuck are you doing?" she spat down the phone.

"OK, I got caught but also got the photos for you."

"I didn't want him to know."

"What do you mean?"

"You fucking idiot. I wanted the evidence and then would deal with it in my own way. It was going to be a slow process. I didn't want him to leave me, just stop dipping his wick elsewhere."

"Well, you can still do that."

"No I can't, you twat. He's left me because he said the trust has gone. And you're fucking responsible for that."

"I think it may have happened anyway if you don't mind me saying Mrs Hearst."

"I do fucking mind, I mind very fucking much. Fuck you and your money. You're not getting it. Sue me."

And so to the dead rock star. This case was unique because I didn't know who my client was. So the first email just said:

Vance Monaco was no accident, he was murdered.

I duly ignored it. You wouldn't believe the number of nutters who got in touch. Some recurring themes, like the flat earth conspiracists, always tickled my funny bone. Despite all the evidence dating back to the ancient Greeks and actual live pictures from space looking back at the round earth, they still believe we live on a disc-shaped planet. They dismiss all the modern facts as cover-ups going all the way to the top of most Western governments. This is between their shock therapy sessions, where their testicles were hooked up to the mains in the asylum. Other interesting possible jobs included the case of Paul McCartney secretly dying in 1966 and Elvis not being brown bread but running a B&B in Skegness as a landlady called Elvira. When I got letters on actual paper, they were always written in different coloured inks with lots of underlining and circling of words, really making sure their unhinged personalities shone through. Both the paper and electronic forms of communication usually had lots of random words in capitals, shouting in type.

The second e-mail was from the lottery. I'd been playing the lottery online for years. It was so much easier and meant I didn't need to go to the corner shop where some idiot had filled in pages of lines on numerous tickets but had got one wrong. I never played the same numbers because that caused more trouble than it was worth. If you did that, the digits became printed on your brain. You knew them instantly and could recite them in your sleep and as long as you played those numbers every single week, there wasn't a problem. A friend of mine, Julia, had played the lottery with the same numbers since it first began. Her birthday was 12th August, so two numbers were 12 and 8. Her mother married on 25th September, so 25 was the next one. Her dog had four spots on his nose, so 4 had to be included. The number of boyfriends she'd had an orgasm with was 1. For the last number, she really pulled it out of the bag. Her brother had been born with three nipples. To redress his terrible time at school for such an affliction, 3 was the final key to unlocking countless riches. These numbers were set in stone and she never wavered. One Saturday morning, she got a call from a very old friend who had just had a bit of bad news. Being a kindly soul, Julia offered to meet her for a consolation session over lunch. But, after two bottles of wine, time recognition went out of the window. She couldn't get away as the friend kept breaking out in uncontrollable sobbing. When it got to three bottles, all Julia could do was stumble into a cab, return home to throw up and wake up on Sunday morning on the sofa. After a bath, the Sunday slobs on to get the papers. Whilst walking back to her flat, carrying a small rainforest in a newspaper, she glanced at the lottery results on the front page of one of the rags. Immediately halting in her tracks, she dropped everything on the ground and stood for a few moments before picking up the papers and staring at those results. They were her numbers. They were the numbers that she had played every draw for 10 years. They were also the numbers that she didn't have a ticket for. Because of her inebriation the day before, the ticket hadn't been bought. Many months later, Julia told me she went to work every day, knowing she shouldn't be doing that. She shouldn't be getting the tube, going to a job she hated, and working with people she loathed. I could only begin to fathom the hell she was going through. If it had been me, I'd have turned into a basket case, constantly muttering to myself about how my friend was an evil witch and how she'd ruined my life. No, a lucky dip was the only way to go. Allowing the numbers to be picked randomly by the lottery took all that pressure away.

The subject line of the e-mail read: *News about your lottery ticket.* The first time I got one, I almost had a heart attack. Seeing it was from the lottery and there was some good news supposedly. My pulse was racing and I started to feel lightheaded. The text in the body of the e-mail informed me that there was exciting news about my ticket and all I needed to do was follow the link. When I clicked, it read:

Your ticket has won. Click on 'My Account' to see how much.

I was sweating, thinking that it was the moment that would change my life forever. It was difficult to click the mouse; I was shaking so much. Then, as the next page revealed itself, I took a huge deep breath.

CONGRATULATIONS. You have won £10.

Then came another message from the same address as the first - rocklegend@gmail.com :

I want to engage you to investigate this case. I have deposited 30k in your business account. There will be another 30 once the job is done. You can try to find out who I am but will never succeed. Just accept the case.

Interest piqued, I checked the company account and there it was, a big fat 30 thousand payment in. I'd never ever had that amount of money on the plus side of my balance. Sadly though, it took my credit to only £2,001 thanks to my crippling overdraft. I was truly awful with money. Most normal people will look at what they've got at the beginning of the month and budget the rest of the days to fit that. I always just started spending, only to realise a few weeks into the month I had no cash to take me to the next paycheque. When I was employed, this was difficult enough. Still, as a freelance PI, my child's grasp of money management really wasn't the best way to approach the matter.

Under my investigator's licence, I was duty-bound to look into all new customers. I had to ensure they weren't planning to blow us up or hadn't gained their income by supplying enough Colombian marching powder to fuel a music awards ceremony. Also, much of my work came from police forces up and down the country, so I had to make sure there wasn't a headline like 'Private dick in drug ring scandal.' The PayPal reference was the same as the email address. My search brought absolutely nothing. I exhausted various avenues, contacts with my former police colleagues, and of course the all-knowing Google. All to no avail.

4

It was time to make my way to the pub to mull this conundrum. I always found the warm embrace of a local boozer, and of course, the beer contained therein helped me figure certain things out. I lived in a part of London typically described as a 'complete shithole'. Although all the articles about the area always said 'up and coming'. That was just papering over what was a rundown, pisspoor and sometimes violent neighbourhood. As I turned the corner by the tube entrance, a white van drove through a huge puddle covering me and my cream summer suit in dirty water. The cigarette I'd just lit was now wet mush. When faced with such a situ, I had no option but to question the driver's heritage. He skidded to a stop.

"Piss off Prince Harry!" The neanderthal driver shouted out of the window. Then, he made the universally accepted clenched fist movement to reinforce his point. "Fucking wanker!" He then wheelspun off with way too many revs in the engine. Watching across the road was Tommy the tramp, sitting where he always did, drinking the most potent cider known to man. I deposited my regular contribution to his alcohol fund into the tin.

"Prince Harry, brilliant!" he muttered, laughing even more hysterically than usual, showcasing the teeth he'd grown in Coca-Cola. I was pretty sure his accent was Scottish but the years of abuse he'd inflicted on his mouth and brain, meant the vocal range had become a universal, non-specific slur. Yes, I had red hair and a beard but thought I bore no resemblance at all to the Prince formerly known as Prince. I made a mental note to question my standard donation next time. A tramp, extracting the Michael out of me, one for the achievements post on the fridge door.

My local was *The Oak & Saw,* a.k.a. *The Open Sore* because its decor was unchanged from the 70s and a place where Guantanamo prisoners would refuse the food. Bob and I were at what the landlord, Roger, called 'the quiet table'. I had no idea why the publican referenced it thus because every table was quiet, and all had a sticky surface that could be used to trap elephants.

"You piss yourself?" Bob asked, looking at my wet trousers. He was a professional driver with Popeye arms (including the tattoos) and a face like he'd run into a wall. A low wall though; he was only 5ft 2 inches tall. 'Bullshit Bob' was his nickname in the pub because he embellished every story with unbelievable nonsense. Some of his classics included a shoot-out with the FBI after a child was kidnapped, confronting terrorists who had taken over an office building, and driving a hitman to various contracts. If you think those stories sound familiar, you'd be right. Action movies were all Bob watched and so he just repeated the plots in his tales. That aside, I had used him often in my investigations. He was connected with people who'd rather stab me than talk to me, so Bob found things out in exchange for cash. He had his thoughts on my dilemma.

"Look, if you wanna wash moolah, you're not going to send it to the filf now are ya!" Even though I'd not been 'filf' for a couple of years, he still couldn't let it lie. He did have a point though. With my history, I'd be a bit of a risky punt for some undesirable to rinse ill-gotten gains. "No, keep schtum and take the folding. Better than a kick in the balls." He crossed his arms in a job-done sort of way. Still mulling the ethics of the situ, an email came in on my phone. The phone pinged with that annoying sound. Every time it did that, I reminded myself to ask BB how to make that silent. It was from the tax case officer who had it in for me. The 40k tax bill was going legal. My money management skills also failed spectacularly when it came to tax. No one likes paying tax but I never had the money put aside to settle the bill and thus spent most of my time ignoring the threatening letters that came through the letterbox. I needed the money or else I'd be spending my time behind bars (not the good ones), avoiding picking up the soap in the showers. I was going to take the risk that my *Know Your*

Customer processes had gone for a burton. My decision made on the case, we then got on to other matters.

"So how'd it go with that date?" Little did Bob know, this was a very pertinent question. I'd always been useless with women. I wasn't shy and would happily start a conversation with a brick. I just lacked any sense of confidence with actually attracting the opposite sex. This flaw was a tad of a hinderance. A man confident in himself, in his strengths and qualities, without being arrogant, was supposedly the desired vibe women wanted from men. Of course, there were times this disability was bypassed but even when that happened, events usually conspired against me. For example, the time I was on holiday with my old mate Jerry, when in our twenties. All sinew, bouffant hair and not an ounce of fat on our bodies. We were staying at his parent's place in Ibiza. Every year whilst at university, we were lucky enough to spend a month there in the summer, getting blind drunk and dabbling in the odd bit of naughty stuff in outdoor nightclubs. One day, particularly hung over and having only had a few hours of sleep, we were in a bar for the afternoon snifter that would kick it all off again. Our cotton wool heads and the desire to vomit vanished instantly when two beautiful women wandered into view. They were almost angel-like and it seemed as though they were bathed in a sunshine glow that no one else in the bar had. It turned out that they were also very nice. Most girls would have been put off by two dishevelled guys salivating, but they actually said hello. Not quite believing these two creatures from Venus were actually talking to us, we didn't respond, just stared. The second hello finally jolted us out of our stupor.

"Do you know a good local restaurant where we can go to lunch?" the brunette asked. We stumbled through a recommendation, gibbering like idiots.

"We'll go there tomorrow and it would be great if you guys are there. We could join up for lunch," the blonde said in perfect English with a supremely sexy French accent. Of course, it wasn't every day that two of the hottest girls we'd ever seen wanted to meet up for lunch.

"Absolutely," we both said, trying to retain some sort of cool.

"Bye then. Look forward to seeing you tomorrow, " the blonde said chirpily.

"À demain," I said as they floated out of the bar into the sunshine.

"À demain? How the fuck did you remember that? You were useless at French in school." Jerry inquired.

"Je suis maintenant un homme de l'Europe, mon ami," I said as we both raised our glasses of white Rioja in a smug manner that was more than a little tainted with disbelief as to what had just happened.

The next day, again with crippling hangovers, we decided to take Jerry's dad's speedboat out for a spin pre-lunch with the goddesses. It was no more than a large rowing boat with a small engine on the back, but we never failed to have fun pottering aimlessly around the sea, thinking we were the dog's knackers. After half an hour, the boat broke down a good 20-minute swim from the shore. We called the port and were told they'd send out a rescue boat. However, this was Spain; thus, there was no sense of urgency to come to our aid. After an hour of stomach-churning bobbing on the waves, there was still no sign of rescue. Then, feeling incredibly ill, we were lying on the boat floor when we heard an enormous motor churning. Sitting up expecting to see a rescue boat, we were greeted by the sight of a vast and powerful boat. It was immense. The 'fun' boat on the back of this monster was the same size as the one we were currently languishing in. As it went past, we heard voices.

"Allo, boys!" We looked up to the rear deck and saw the girls from the bar. They were sunbathing and waving down to us. We couldn't help but notice something else. They were naked, their long limbs and breasts glinting in the sun. One guy was driving, sitting perched at the controls with a cocktail in his hand. He looked down at us, raised his glass, winked and then threw the throttle full forward, sending the front of the boat into the air as it sped off. Our nausea from sitting in that boat for over an hour was exacerbated by the massive wake from the monster.

"Naked, " Jerry said, shaking his head as we waved pathetically at the girls heading out to sea. "Fucking naked."

"And the size of that boat. Jesus.'

"Naked. No bikini. Nothing. Nada. Shit.' Jerry was still waving.

"I'm sure that bastard driving it was sneering at us,' I spat.

"Of course he was. Wouldn't you if you were him?' I thought about this for a second and accepted that I would have done exactly the same and would have loved it. Funnily enough, we never saw those girls again. Although there was a question mark over whether they were prostitutes or not, it didn't matter. Back to the date Bob was asking about.

"I thought she was taking a long time in the toilet but then I got a text – from her. It said you might want to order an Uber. I'm already in one," I explained.

"How'd you fuck that up so badly?"

"All I did was question her use of like."

"What?"

"It can be used in two ways. One as a verb, I like wine, or it's mostly used to compare things. Bob looks like a baby troll."

"Oh yeah," he said. "What about this? Colin acts like a giant cock."

5

Music legend Sir Vance Monaco was rock royalty, officially so having been inducted into the rock hall of fame. He'd been the lead singer of *Thunderbolt*, the biggest band of the eighties/ nineties and then a hugely successful solo artist still able to fill up stadiums. Although the gigs were markedly different to the hell-raising days, it was more likely the mothers attending with their daughters who would scream at the presence on stage of the main man. He was the archetypal rock star both in his youth and later in life. In the latter part of his career, he still wore clothes no man close to retirement age should. Amazingly, he still had blonde spikey hair, was never without skin-tight jeans even the kids wouldn't wear, was partial to the odd fur coat and glitter-covered cowboy boots. He moved in the upper echelon of society, as popular with members of the royal family as other A-listers in the entertainment business across the world. That was until on a routine parachute jump he'd done hundreds of times before, he freefell for 14,000 feet, hitting the ground at 200 mph. The effect of this turned the inside of his body into unset jelly.

The police investigation was brief because the overstretched Met lacked the resources or inclination for a long one. They did manage to find that the risers in his parachute had been sliced. Risers are the fabric straps and ring formation that connect the parachute to the body harness. So they are quite an important part of the kit for the person falling through the air. There were two sets, one for the main chute and the other for the backup. The laws of physics meant they were strong enough to withstand the immediate and massive pressure exerted on them when the chute was deployed. This ensured the canopy and parachutist didn't go their separate ways – as happened to Vance. The police knew it was a very sharp implement that did the slicing because forensic tests showed the cuts on both sides of the harness had no fraying at their edges. When Vance pulled the cord of the main chute, he would have looked up to see it deploy minus him. The same thing would have happened with his backup. At this stage, he would have known the only thing going to slow him down was terra firma. The DNA tests on Monaco's jumpsuit, the recovered parachutes, and his equipment found nothing besides his own. There were no other fabrics present anywhere. The upshot was the police came to the opinion that it could've been suicide but with no corroboration and, worse, no real evidence, an accident ruling was their only option.

Where do you start? I was always asked this at parties. There was never the same answer, although a couple of times, when I couldn't be bothered getting into a conversation, I'd say at the beginning. I stopped using that line though having heard myself one night answering a horrible man with halitosis that was singeing my hair each time he bellowed. Even to that walking WMD, I still realised I sounded a complete dickhead. The honest answer was it all depended on instinct, case circumstances and situational awareness. That last particular quality was the overriding force in this case. I was cripplingly hungover from an unplanned 'beer' the previous night. Not just a hangover, one of those ones that render speech and movement something you wish you could do without wanting to Hughie Green. I'd met a mate who was something quite successful in the city. Not just 'quite', he used fifty-pound notes as toilet roll. Not really, but could do if he wanted. I'd known him since school and wondered why I didn't follow his path. He liked money, so said no to uni and went straight into a hedge fund in the square mile. He was retired (not jealous in any way) but still dabbled in the markets for fun. The amount of cash he played around with would have looked after me for the rest of my life. I too liked money but when a kid, no one pointed out that you needed to do the do early rather than getting drunk and trying to get laid at college. And then be very lucky. He lived in the country in some mansion (or the Bahamas in one of his other mansions), so whenever I met him in London, he stayed in the best hotel, took me to the best restaurants and then onto the most exclusive nightclubs. I shuddered to think how much it cost him but when I offered to go down the *Open Sore* for a pint where I could buy the rounds, he always laughed, with tears and all. So cripplingly hung, I couldn't think about where to start. Luckily the client emailed and suggested I speak to Anita Savage first. She was Vance's long-standing PA. I wasn't in the habit of letting unknown employers run my investigation. Still, the situational awareness came in as a phone call was the maximum I could handle from the couch.

In the past, I'd been accused of being harsh and unsympathetic to those who had lost friends and family. It's not that I'd become immune to sympathy. On the contrary, I always felt for the victims' nearest and dearest. It's just that if I carried out my job, and my former job, by turning to mush each time they were interviewed, I wouldn't have said jobs. Miss A. Savage tried to be very helpful but was not in the right place for any meaningful insight. First, the suicide option needed looking at. There was no point embarking on the journey if I could rule out ending his own life at the beginning of the case.

"What do you think his state of mind was like before the jump?" I asked after muted pleasantries were exchanged. It took her an age to get to the answer. I could hear her mouth had gone very dry, which started to grate with me. After years of finding various noises drove me to despair, I discovered a medical disorder present in certain human beings. Misophonia, sometimes called selective sound sensitivity syndrome, is a baffling and bizarre disorder. Medical sites state: 'Patients feel an instantaneous, overwhelming, and uncontrollable rage - often accompanied by physiological responses such as sweaty palms or a racing heart - to certain sounds." When I read that, a weight was lifted from my shoulders. I'd previously thought my inner Victor Meldrew had come out, crotchety for the sake of it. The syndrome had caused break-ups with girlfriends who couldn't deal with my stupid reactions to various noises. My particular triggers were things like sniffing, yawning, something being played loud through a phone speaker (a particular blood boil for that one) and the noise made by lack of moisture in the mouth.

"He loved sky diving. Obsessed with it. He was going to buy another club and a couple of planes before, before..." She broke off her speech and went silent.

"Ms Savage?" I could make out a slight whimper.

"I can't believe he's gone," she whispered.

"I know, very sad but was he depressed in any way?" The whimpering got louder and I realised this sound needed to be added to the list of condition triggers. My instinct told me this should not have been the kickoff interview and it reaffirmed why I never usually allowed the client to dictate first steps.

"Such a lovely man," her emotions went up a notch again, making it difficult for her to talk.

"Ms Savage, I do need to get to the bottom of what happened. When did you last see Mr Monaco?"

"I can't believe you're gone," she sobbed with her words barely audible.

"I know it's tough, but you knew him for years; please try to answer my questions."

"He was so good to us all. Me and my daughter." Full-on wailing ensued.

"Thank you for your time Ms Savage, Goodbye?"

After recovering a couple of days later, I applied some of the damaged grey matter to the details, plus a bit of using the old boys' network. Another old mate from school went into the army at 16; he didn't even bother with A-levels. Adventure and adrenaline were his particular things and boy did he get those in his chosen profession, plus people shooting at him. Still searching for more excitement, he became one of the 'Hereford lot' aka, the SAS. I don't know if you've ever met anyone in the Special Air Service, but they are not what you expect from the movies, i.e. super tall, super buff meatheads. They're affable, intelligent, wiry, ordinary guys on the outside. But behind their eyes, you can see they've done things you can only imagine. You know they've been in situations that would have finished any hardened soldier. Those mofos would gut, fillet and hang you on a washing line using just their little finger while sipping a beer. I digress. He told me that the way risers can be seen on the shoulder of the parachute harness, if someone had sliced them, the cuts needed to be somewhere where they couldn't easily be spotted by the wearer. Intimate knowledge of how a parachute worked was essential if someone other than Vance had cut the risers. If the slashers didn't know what they were doing, Vance would have spotted the tampering when he picked up the parachute in prep for going out.

6

Sir Vance loved to skyfall, as the regular skydiving fraternity called it. *The Flying Aces* was where the deceased did all this particular vertigo-inducing activity. So the first person of genuine interest to interview was the pilot who owned the club and who usually flew Vance on his lunatic missions into the sky to put himself at the mercy of gravity, a couple of straps and a bit of silk. The Aces website was slick. The homepage featured a video that started from behind a pilot seated at the controls of a plane. Clear blue skies filled the windows in front of him. He had the handsome, rugged looks you'd expect of someone who flew a plane for a living, all jaw, overalls, and aviators.

"You wanna fly?" Said the pilot to the camera as he gestured around the cockpit. "Or fly!" and launched himself out of the seat. The camera spun around into the plane as the man, previously at the controls, ran down the fuselage and out the open backside. It followed and the last shot was looking up at the plane they had just exited. Even though it was just a video, my knees went weak as vertigo kicked in. The affliction had gotten so bad that I even had panic attacks on ski chairlifts.

"Don't look at the ground, look at the tops of the trees," my no-fear 11 yr old godson assured me once when having one of these attacks.

"That's the fucking problem, we're level with the tops of the fucking trees," I hollered back. I later apologized to him and his parents once I'd calmed down with a Vin Chaud - the blood of skiing gods. So the idea of jumping out of a perfectly working aeroplane and falling from that height is why the human brain is programmed like that in the first place, so we don't end up like

Vance.

Typically, a company 'about us' page would have all sorts of team members to make themselves look bigger, so even the tea lady would be on there. Doris Miggins, dietitian consultant and lifesaver. This one just featured Mr aviators, who it turned out was the pilot, Clause Walner. I knew it was pronounced with the 'ause' from 'pause' because of another guy with the same spelling, my former Pilates teacher. He got angry when anyone pronounced it Claus (as in mouse). He became former when my long-standing girlfriend ran off with him a year before this case. That act, for me, ruined our relationship, my idea of real love, Pilates, and Santa all in one go. The main picture was him in a cockpit, again, this time facing forward. There were a load of others doing flying stuff. His bio stated that as an ex-air force captain, he was the safest pair of hands if you wanted to learn to fly or skydive. Strangely, he wasn't at the controls that fateful day. In his police interview, the pilot who was - said that he was called last minute to stand in on the flight. The young aviator didn't question the sudden request, after all, as the backup pilot, that's what he was there for. He'd never met Monaco before and up until that morning, he'd been on holiday in Spain with his girlfriend.

I met Clause at Knowles Hill Aerodrome. It had been one of the main bases for Spitfires fighting the Battle of Britain as it was one of the closest airfields to the English Channel. So many of the few to be thanked by so many, as Churchill said, launched from there. So many also didn't come back. Surviving the war and then the modernisation of the world, it had stayed put. It was still pretty active as a leisure airfield. There was a museum in memory of all the young men the took off and never landed. One of the pictures was of Vance on Remembrance Sunday with the only surviving three flyboys stationed there and went up for so many defence missions against the Luftwaffe. As I pulled up in my car club motor (a brilliant invention if ever there was one) to the gate, a teenager in a high-vis vest looked so pleased that he'd started his shift without the smoke. Everyone was wearing yellow vests, even protestors and muggers. It gave them all a level of legitimacy that never got questioned. 'Oh you're wearing a high vis, so you must be official. Crack on, don't worry about me.' He looked up from his phone as I pulled up.

"I'm here to see Clause Walner," I proffered.

"You can see who you fucking like mate," he said, shrugged and went back to his phone.

A long single-track road from the gate led to what looked like hangars. I arrived at what I assumed was the car park. However, it was hard to tell if it was for cars as there were various small panes of different ages and conditions everywhere. Finally, I spotted the plane from the video. A Twin Otter, the most beloved skydiving jump plane in the world, according to my research. Pilots adored them because they're so manoeuvrable and responsive with twin propellor engines. Skydivers loved them as they had 22 seats that speedily lifted jumpers to 13,500 feet in under 15 minutes. The steps led down from the fuselage onto the tarmac below. There he was, at the top of them. Dressed in a non-necessary green jumpsuit, aviator sunglasses and hair like Iceman from Top Gun (the original and only one) - Clause.

Once out of the car, he made me wait at the foot of the steps, despite me shouting his name and waving. He looked around, posing as though David Bailey was doing the photoshoot. I instantly thought he was a dickhead. Eventually, he started his descent, so slowly and purposefully, I was minded to start up and meet him, but then he would have won. I wasn't going to concede so early. I imagined he'd been waiting at the top for hours before I arrived just so he could do the action man bit. After finally arriving at the bottom of the steps, he kept his sunglasses on as he shook my hand. This confirmed my initial suspicion of him being a right c u next Tuesday. He squeezed way too hard, trying to assert his manliness. I found myself responding in kind, which wasn't usually me. It became clear that he wasn't going to yield first. To save us both from gurning until dark, I let go. He looked as though he'd just been made heavyweight champion of the world. I know what most women would say about this stag-rutting behaviour, which involved holding up the little finger of one hand.

"So why should I talk to you? You're just a private dick," he said, still basking in his triumph.

"Oh, that old one. Claus, do you mind if I call you that?" I'd gone for the irritation straight out of the blocks, hoping it would rile.

"I do."

"Well, Claus, I've spoken with DI in charge of the case. That's Detective Inspector to you." He took his sunglasses off dramatically and squinted at me like he needed a number two. "Although they have ruled it as an accident, they take my investigation into account and reopen the case to pursue any new leads if necessary. So as far as you're concerned, I'm a copper."

"Huh," he grunted

"How often did he like to jump?"

"Lots."

"And who did he jump with most?"

"Manager."

"Isn't someone supposed to check his gear beforehand?" I'd discovered that all jumps require someone to check the other's kit before throwing themselves out to the mercy of physics.

"Yep." It was like trying to milk a chicken.

"Who did the day he died?"

"Dunno didn't do that jump."

"But you always did his jumps. Is that not true?"

"Nope. Didn't fly that day."

"Jesus wept! OK, why didn't you fly Vance's final jump even though you'd done every single one before?"

"Rota issues."

"Is there anything else you think may be pertinent?"

"Nah."

"You've been so incredibly helpful, thank you."

There was no point going on with Top Gun.

Back at my flat, I was greeted by the usual horrific smell of cat poo. The feline was called Bubbles; it was the ex-girlfriend's, so named because she was a Michael Jackson superfan, the girlfriend not the cat obviously. I was a dog man but because of our lack of a child, I agreed to get the ginger tabby as a substitute. I hated it with a passion but tolerated it when we were together for love and a peaceful life. Unfortunately, in the ex's haste to shack up with Mr Pilates, she lost her devotion and left it behind shouting I could keep the little effer. So I was stuck with something that produced something Sadam Hussian would have wanted, three times a day. However, one thing Bubbles did provide when it considered me worthy of its time, was a sounding board that allowed me to unload.

"I didn't like the pilot." The cat just looked at me with contempt. "Never trust a Clause. Rota issues doesn't add up." It started licking its bottom, the cat equivalent of 'talk to the hand'. "He had the knowledge to cut those risers and was there at the airfield on the day of the jump, just didn't fly the plane. After all those jumps together, then no jump together and then musician shuffles off this mortal coil." Bubbles jumped off the sofa, ambled to the litter tray, and deposited her feelings on the matter in it. I nearly threw up and swore to look at her diet and change what she was eating.

I asked Bob to do some digging on our friend Clause

7

Date time again, this time a blind one. I didn't have any problems with blind dates. I was cool with meeting new people; for some reason, people always opened up to me, spurting out stuff they should never be telling strangers. I had a smiley, welcoming and expressive face, I was told by a chugger once and why would they lie? This had been set up by the sister of a friend. I had a slight incident on my way to meet her at the cocktail bar. There are three sets of gangs in London. The ones knifing each other over drug turf wars or beef (not the bovine kind), the militant Lycra-clad cyclists speeding through red lights like they were in MadMax and seagulls. These rottweilers with wings roamed the skies of London with impunity thanks to the Wildlife and Countryside Act 1801 which made them a protected species. Having long given up on what they're supposed to eat (fish) and where they're supposed to live (the sea), it's all in the name. They'd been allowed to populate the capital city in alarming numbers. Their diet now consisted not of ice creams nabbed from unsuspecting day-trippers on a pier much to the amusement of everyone, but ravaging rubbish bags, bins, dead rodents (yes, seagulls eat meat) and handbag dogs.

As I approached our meeting venue, I heard the loud screech of a gull, looked up and was engulfed in a wingspan like something out of Game of Thrones. I tried to beat it off but had to beat a retreat into the pub next door to the cocktail bar. I ran in and burst through the doors to a sparsely populated spit and sawdust place. The *Open Sore* was a hole, but this place pipped it for the worst pub in London. There were three old men in the corner discussing not much at all. A guy on the other side was wearing bright orange trousers and a top of the construction kind. The barman was a very bored teenager whose t-shirt suggested he'd rather be consuming mind-enhancing drugs than being in a toilet of a pub with old men. He'd even given up talking to the guy standing at the bar who seemed to be a regular. They had clearly ran out of things to say to each other every day, every week.

"Seagull?" asked the guy at the bar as the door closed behind me.

"They're big," I said, slightly out of breath from trying to beat off the bird away from around my head. Two of the old guys in the corner with walking sticks by their side held up hard hats with 'Crossrail' on them and pointed at the guy on his own in the construction gear. On closer inspection, his overalls had 'Crossrail' all over them, and he too had the same hard hat. I was early for the date, so thought a sharpener wouldn't hurt and ordered a pint at the bar. The problem was I had to endure the funny guy trying to make conversation. There was always a funny guy in a pub who thought they were hilarious but were just ball-crushingly dull.

"Did you know that they communicate with each other, although usually they're just saying where they can shit." said the funny guy. As he was wittering on, still not getting my hint, the teenager pointed to my head in a grossly underwhelming way. I touched my forehead and looked at my fingers. There was blood on them. The gull had caught me. Retreating to the toilet, I splashed water from the sink over my head, which acted as a dye and spread around the rest of the barnet. I managed to stem the bleeding using techniques I'd seen in documentaries. It was all about pressure on the wound that made the blood cells coagulate. All those war movies were right; pressure really does work. I downed the half pint and got out of there.

Fully restored to normality, I sat at the restaurant bar awaiting my companion. I hated being late for anything and when it came to dates, it was always the man's prerogative to be early and the woman's prerogative to be late. I didn't make the rules; they were fine by me. My friend had given me the usual blurb for these things: 'She's so lovely, she's so beautiful, you guys would so get on, etc.' They never explained that the person in question had just gotten out of somewhere dealing with personality disorders, including eating ones. When she arrived, a sense of disappointment washed over me. I'm no George Clooney but really, what was my friend thinking? So the plan was a drink, then I'd have to go because I needed urgent attention to something or other. We had a few drinks, actually 5, as she turned out to be lovely, funny and plu (people like us). The problem was there was no attraction on either side. It's why online dating never worked. Until you look someone in the eye, feel their physical presence, you have no idea if there is any chemistry. There was none here – on both sides. We both could tell it, but we were having fun. These good vibes ended when I sneezed with force. It wasn't the actual sneeze that was the problem but the pressure exerted on what was supposedly a sealed wound. I blew my nose and apologised, only to look up and see her go deathly white. I'd seen dead bodies go purple but never a living human being go translucent. I realised the blood had started trickling down my forehead again and tried to wipe it away, which only spread it around the forehead. That's when her eyes rolled back and she fell backwards off the bar stool, disappearing like a sack of coal being thrown. Seeing my bloody hands and forehead with a woman unconscious on her back, the rest of the people in the bar panicked. It was a few months after a horrific terrorist attack just round the corner where a machete-wielding lunatic hacked at whatever he could see. To say people were spooked was the understatement of the century. I remember seeing a security team member outside the door rush in and rugby tackle me. The next thing I can recall was being in a police station interview room. It took them a couple of hours to realise I was just an idiot and not some religious hardliner embarking on jihad against the good folk of London.

The next day, having avoided a terror-related arrest, thoughts turned to Monaco's manager, Edon Thanisi. According to his biography, he first met the band in a pub in north London shortly after arriving in the U.K. from Albania. The band was on a bender; after four hours of pace drinking, something I'd rather prided myself on, Vance jumped on their table to demonstrate his party trick. He called it the flamingo and it involved him putting one leg behind his head whilst pulling out his penis through his zip- that was the bird's beak, by the way. He fell onto the next-door table, smashing all their glasses, and after staggering up, he tried to fight the now enraged drinkers. Edon calmed the situation by removing Vance from the fray and buying a couple of rounds for the whole table. Even though the punters still wanted to rip Vance's head off, they agreed. The next day, the band said they needed a manager, and Edon told them he'd be the right guy for the job. That was a deal.

As an unknown manager with an unknown band, he did everything needed on every level. There was the stuff generally reserved for the lowest ranking runner, like drug runs, booze runs, trying to pull groupies out of the small crowds, fights, unblocking toilets, more drug runs, and fielding phone calls from suspicious girlfriends. Then there was the higher-level stuff you'd expect a manager to do, negotiating contracts with venues, trying to get the band signed with a record label, and implementing a marketing/PR strategy.

Once he finally got them signed, things went ballistic. *Thunderbolt* rose to fame and fortune very quickly, as did Thanisi. Various character traits slowly came to the fore. First was a calculating sense of retribution. One example the biographer gave was when the band was staying in the A-list *Henderson* in Los Angeles. Monaco threw a TV out of the 15th-floor window. He thought their room was on the poolside of the hotel, and considering it was 2am, the TV would land harmlessly with a big splash. They were in fact on the street side of the hotel and the set flattened a dog owned by an insomniac who always walked her at that time. The lawsuit was settled with the dog owner, but the hotel group banned them from visiting all their hotels in the world forever. Incensed by a perceived snub, injustice against the band, and a personal insult by the hotel group, Thanisi found out who the person was who banned them. Someone kidnapped the guy's beloved alpacas, videoed themselves petting them, and then shooting them. The vids were sent to the distraught hotel director with a caption on the bottom saying 'Retribution'. Thanisi claimed to know nothing about the incident; he didn't know anybody like that and condemned such vile acts. The police found no evidence of his involvement. No shooters or even dead alpacas were ever found.

Another characteristic that became prevalent was a very short fuse. His temper became legendary in the industry and was known for being the biggest, toughest, hardest mofo out there.

Those were the days before safe work practices were introduced. So his despicable behaviour towards people he deemed lower than him was never questioned. One example was when the band arrived for a particular concert. Backstage there was the wrong type of M&M's in bowls in the dressing rooms. He threw them all over the floors, called the runners in, and told them to get on the floor and eat the offending sweets directly off the ground whilst he shouted at them. It was fair to say that he'd never get a fair play award if he were a football team.

Thunderbolt split up in '95 because the drummer, Clint, had a new girlfriend. She tried to take the group in another musical direction. That was Thanasi's territory, not hers. He signed Vance up as a solo client and then, being such a nice guy, made it his mission to ruin Clint's career and life in general. The drummer joined a new band but ended up in jail for sex with a minor. Clint claimed the girl had said she was 21 years old. The judge ruled that because she spoke only Albanian, Clint was lying. He was released a month later when investigators discovered that the girl was indeed 21 years old, fluent in English and the whole thing had been a scam. On release, he set up a turtle rescue charity on an island in the middle of the Indian Ocean and never played music again. The girlfriend OD'd in some squat in Manchester. He was next to interview, but all this research had exhausted me and a pint was needed

8

On my way to Thanisi's office, I passed Tommy but didn't do my usual deposit of funds for his surgical spirit strength libation this time. This wasn't because I was miffed at him taking the piss out of me, even though I was a bit. I simply didn't have any change on me, nor did it seem anyone else. Everyone had become used to paying for everything with a tap and those who used the folding were either crooks or didn't have bank accounts – or both. I had an idea for homeless charities. They could use the money given to them to do something more useful than helping the poor unfortunates sell *The Big Issue*. If they set up a payment system and gave every homeless person a tappy card receiver, the amount of money the poor souls would get daily would multiply by 5 or 10 times. Then the charity could monitor how the money was spent, ensuring it didn't go to the aforementioned guys with no accounts in exchange for drugs. This monitoring would enable them to implement programmes if they noticed a regular payment for meth. This brilliant idea hadn't made it out of my mind, but my lack of patronage seemed to vex Tommy somewhat.

"You just fuck'n pissed I called you that royal dickhead," he muttered. How did a Scottish tramp pick up the US version of 'pissed', i.e. annoyed and not blind drunk? I was pretty sure he wasn't big on popular culture and had never seen an episode of *Keeping up with the Kardashians*. To be fair to him though, nor had I. My blood pretty much boiled to cardiac arrest levels when I saw trailers for the series in between documentaries or history programmes. I read plenty of articles about their influence on young minds, making these viewers lazy gobshites who only ever wanted to be famous as their job. Anything else they weren't interested in, like hard work. I did have to give it to those vacuous, self-obsessed, publicity-seeking, moronic 'stars'. They were rich though. Proper private aviation rich.

Edon's domain of work was Soho, the media capital of London. I'd always liked the area as it usually meant excessive consumption, debauchery and a good time. The bars, restaurants, clubs, dive strip bars, theatres and swanky hotels presented a veritable smorgasbord of entertainment to consume. It was once said, 'If you're tired of New York, you're tired of life!' This applied to Soho too, although the drug addicts had become quite a severe problem. Alba Management, his company, was up a crooked staircase in one of the old Victorian houses on Wardour Street. Like the tardis, a vast modern glass and brilliant furniture reception opened up from the narrow staircase. While waiting to be called in, I glanced down at my feet to notice I'd put one brown and one black shoe on when getting dressed in the dark. They immediately became like vices, squeezing my feet and forcing all the blood up my legs. I couldn't let Edon see this sartorial faux pas as it would've given him an upper hand in the powerplay game these interviews involve. Luckily, when I entered the office, he was on the phone in a glass-walled break-out room. He had his back to me, enabling me to get in front of his desk without being spotted. The first thing that struck me was the jacket. Wow! Just Wow! It was a white blazer with a red velvet collar and black feathers sewn all over, which fluttered in the aircon, making him shimmer like Shirley Bassey. It takes a very confident man to wear that hideous thing, not as a bet. His accent was strangely not Eastern European.

"Listen you bald dickwad, I will shit in your mouth and then cut your head off with nail scissors if you renege on this deal," he shouted. There was a short pause while he listened to the person on the other end. "NO! Fuck you. I look after A-listers all over the world. Do the fucking deal." He ended the call and came into the office.

"Sorry, work you know how it is right?" a rhetorical question. I managed to shake his hand without him seeing over the desk at my mis-dressed feet.

"Just trying to do a deal with a real superstar." Before I even enquired who, he said, "Sorry, I'm under NDA." He sat down and fixed me with a steely, squinted look. "So, who are you working for?"

"Can't say I'm afraid."

"Why not?"

"Client confidentiality."

"Ah well, two can play at that game. That policy also applies to my client relationship."

"Ex-client."

"His business interests are still my responsibility and will be forever."

"If my findings uncover foul play and I think you've got something to hide, I will recommend the police insert themselves into your life like a hamster in Soho."

"I'm starting to not like you, Mr Todd."

"I get that a lot. So could he have killed himself

"How would I know?"

"You've been his manager since time began. Some would say you're closer than his family. So you should know if he was depressed or worried."

"We weren't friends. He was my client; you could even say we didn't like each other. It was strictly business, I made him money which made me money."

"But you jumped together regularly, that's not business?"

"If my client says jump, I jump -metaphorically and physically. It's what managers do."

"How would you describe his state of mind recently?"

"Fucking nuts."

"How so?" Thanisi sighed heavily. "He'd become paranoid, got involved in conspiracy theories."

"Like what?"

"All sorts of shit, but the real obsession became hackers. He believed they would access his life via wi-fi devices and that one day, he'd get an email showing him in a gimp suit hanging from a harness."

"He had particular sexual tastes then?"

"All the weird shit. After decades of getting all he wanted in that department, the norm became boring, so the abnormal became the norm." I was writing this down in the notebook but not sure why. "So, afraid they'd hack him, he took all the Bluetooth and Wi-Fi devices off the network at his home." This rang true with me. Someone I knew in state security had told me the cyber-attack extorting our NHS with a virus came from an internet-enabled fridge. I couldn't understand why someone would want a 'connected' fridge in the first place. Eventually, the fridges would rise up, trapping their owners in the walk-in compartments, playing death music via Alexa as the humans suffocated on that Pak Choi that had been over-ordered - by the fridges.

"He got so caught up in it, the crazy motherfucker was even changing his will, leaving the lot to some conspiracy theory nutjob group so they could continue their valuable work."

"What was the name of this group?"

"Crap!"

"I'm only asking."

"Conspiracy Realities Are Plenty."

"Oh, right. Did you say anything to him about this?"

"Of course I did. He didn't like that. No one tells Vance Monaco he was batshit crazy, so we had a few words."

"Did you check his parachute before the jump?"

"No, he said it had already been done at home."

"Why didn't you notice there was a problem during the jump?"

"Cloudy conditions. Now I've got a very important call to make, goodbye Mr Todd." I got up and started to make my way out, keeping close to my side of the desk so as not to give away my footwear horror.

"One final question, why didn't you call the police after he hit the ground?"

"We didn't know what happened until his chutes drifted down. When we eventually found him, I assumed one of the staff would call them." Thanisi leaned back in his chair, put his feet up on the desk, and sneered at me as I walked out. "You do realize you're wearing one brown and one black shoe, right?" Bastard! When I looked at him, his face turned back to the steely stare, "Be careful Mr Todd. There might be some nasty people involved in all this. We wouldn't want anything nasty to happen to you, now would we." He then picked up his phone and started dialling.

9

Where else to go after dealing with such a man but the pub. Bob and I were talking to another couple of regulars. They were the most earnest of north Londoners you would ever meet. All fair trade, right on causes and environmentalism. For example, recycling was a particular bugbear of theirs. They were meticulous to the point of being dictatorial about it. However, like most who follow 'the science' (something that was usually found out in all forms eventually), they never questioned whether their diligence was worth it or not and what they were trying to achieve. As such, they were blissfully unaware that our particular council couldn't handle the amount of 'good' waste gleefully sorted into varying bags and bins by its residents. The borough did want to build a massive facility to do this, but objections from environmentalists who'd found a family of grey spotted toads on the site scuppered the plans. So the good folk at the council decided to abdicate any responsibility and shipped it all off to countries that couldn't give a fig about how to dispose of the different types of rubbish. Great big container ships carried all the plastic, cardboard, paper and various other types of stuff. They were saving the planet by giving the problem to countries in South East Asia and India, who gleefully disposed of it in a manner that would make Greta scowl as if her life depended on it. The wife was something in education; we never knew what because a hazy fog would descend on the listener whenever she started telling anyone about her chosen career. She had the most boring monotone voice ever doled out by the creator. It could stun a charging rhino into sleep at fifty paces. He was a GP, and once you got past whatever socialist agenda he was pushing at the time, he was actually quite funny, albeit with a certain poshness.

"Fuck'n liberty. I was there for six fuck'n hours before some tosser sent me off saying there was nuffink wrong with me." Bob was recounting a story of his last visit to A&E.

"Bob, never go into hospital in the months of August and February,' the doctor said. "August is a bad month because all the consultants have buggered off on holiday. They leave the juniors to man the pumps."

"Off to their fuck'n villas no doubt," Bob said. It was August.

"February is not a good month because that's when hospitals have a fresh intake of newbies and all the other juniors are rotated. So you could be in for an op on your throat only to find they've lobbed off one of your balls."

"I was lucky then."

"Unless you've been run over by a bus, avoid those two months in an NHS hospital like you would a hooker with a cold sore." Sage words indeed. The couple left.

"Do you know anything about the wife?" I asked.

"You don't?"

"Haven't got that far yet."

"Posh bird, bit of a royal."

"I don't follow the royals."

"You don't follow anything. Fuck knows how you do your job." Bob took a big gulp of his pint as he looked around but didn't get to swallow because it was spat out all over me in the sort of reaction like his good lady wife had walked into the pub naked.

"What the?" I questioned in shock.

"I need to talk to you Mr Todd," came a clipped lady's voice from behind me. Bob, still in amazement, quickly moved off to the bar and joined a couple of other regulars – Roids and Sequins. The former was a bodybuilder, a terrible one. Being the shape of a pipe cleaner as a kid, he vowed to bulk up. With his surname being Jones, he was tired of the nickname Skindiana Bones. On going to uni, he frequented the gym every day. It was either that or get ratarsed as most first-year students did. The problem was physiology. His body refused to take the bait and never responded to all the weights and workouts. He started taking every supplement, protein shake and anything else useless the health industry flogged him. He returned home for the summer at the end of the first year. All his friends still called him pipey (cleaner), and no one commented that he'd filled out because he hadn't. The second year, he got to know some of the gym cocks. They were the guys who spent an inordinate amount of time looking at themselves in the mirror at the gym. They did this when doing a set, shouting way too loudly at the exertion, looking like they were having a nasty bowel movement. They also flexed things in between as they strutted around admiring themselves. Yes, they were big, but man, did they want everyone to know it. The other thing about gym cocks was that many of them were using enhancers, as did Roids. Not the over-the-counter stuff but things that were utilising the properties some clever chemist had put into pills and injections. These had the effect of permanently expanding the muscles like Popeye eating spinach. The problem was that these illegal substances also turned their brains into Olive Oyl's. By the time Roids wound up frequenting the *Open Sore*, he'd stopped doing them, but that didn't hinder the creation of a good nickname. The latter gent was an ex-ice-skating dancer turned nightclub doorman. He'd been very talented. With his partner, they were tipped for Olympic gold and fame not seen since Torvill and Dean. Then at a GB Olympic team qualifying event, skulduggery took place. Their main rivals, a particularly nasty pair of bitter gobdaws, weren't going to lose that event and miss out on going to the upcoming winter games. Unlike a particular US skater, they didn't just get someone to bash someone's knee in; they were more devious than that. They paid one of the team technicians (very down on his luck) to remove a number of screws that attached the blade to the boot from Sequins' kit. Halfway through the routine, he went into a Triple Axel (a jump with three turns in the air), and as he landed, the pressure snapped both blades on the skates. He broke his ankle badly enough to never be able to skate again professionally. The rivals and the guy that did the deed were convicted of ABH and got a suspended sentence. Sadly for Roids, Sequins was naturally built like a brick outhouse, emphasising that we're all made in different moulds, whether we like it or not. So being that body type, he went into door work and UFC. He loved both. This rabble all had their backs to me, but I knew they were listening intently. An elegant and angular woman sat down in front of me. Her shiny jet-black hair was pulled back in a ponytail that stretched her skin so tightly her face looked like a football with a balloon stretched over it

"And you are?" I heard a muffled 'Jesus' from Bob.

"I'm Lady Monaco." That took me aback. Usually, I'd have to chase people to talk to them but here, the victim's ex-wife was plonking herself right in front of me. So I asked how she found me.

"My brother had you followed, I'm surprised you didn't notice?

"Porot's on the case," Bob said to the others. Because he left school aged 7, he never got to do French and so couldn't pronounce 'Poirot'. Out of the corner of my eye, I could see the three of them get the shoulder movement from trying not to laugh overtly.

"Your brother being?" A legitimate question I thought.

"Edon."

"Edon Thanisi, from Albania?"

She explained, "He was the family bad boy when a teenager. Pa-pa sent him away to stay with friends there. He came back with a new name (our surname is Fortesque) and persona. He's always very suspicious, particularly as you didn't tell him who'd hired you. Anyway, he introduced me to Vannie." She could see my questioning look. "My husband," she said with complete dismissive ease.

"Oh yes, yes of course. Did the two of them get on?"

"They'd known each other for so long and what with all the shenanigans, they, of course, had fallings out. Edon wasn't happy about Britney as he could see it really upset me."

"Britney?"

"Clearly, as a brilliant detective, you know about her?" I did try to hide my look of who the hell was that, tilted my head to one side, nodded, and went to pick up a coaster to nonchalantly fiddle with. Unfortunately, it was stuck to the table.

"Jesus, even Tommy knows her," Bob said to the others with more hidden laughter at the bar.

"That little, classless trollop he was making the beast of two backs with," she hissed. I needed to change the narrative. It was supposed to be me doing the investigating after all.

"Now we've dealt with the how you're here; what about the why Lady Monaco?"

"I've lost my husband."

"But I thought you were separated?"

"He was still my husband and I wanted to meet the person poking around in our family business. Who's paying you to do this?"

"I can't tell you as I genuinely don't know."

"Isn't that against regulations?" She clearly had done some homework.

"It's fine. You let me worry about that."

As she got up, she said, "I suggest you check Instagram, Britney Chalmers." Again, I tried to reassert control that I'd lost.

"Do you skydive Lady Monaco?" She looked at me like I'd just said Wholefoods was a complete scam and all the produce came from an illegal rubbish tip.

"Why on earth would I jump out of a perfectly working aeroplane." Then she gave me a look down her nose which I have to say, was quite effective. "You know who you look like?"

"George Clooney right?" There was even what looked like a

slight crease on the corner of the mouth indicating a smile. With all the Botox, she could have been laughing hysterically for all I knew. "People don't like you prying into their business." She said.

"A professional hazard."

"Be careful about poking sleeping bears with sticks, Mr Todd. It makes them attack." And then she was gone.

Bob sat down, shaking his head.

"Ahh, she had you on toast son."

"I got the info I was looking for."

"If you say so Porot."

"I think you'll find it's pronounced Poirot."

"And I think you'll find it's pronounced fuck off!"

10

I arranged to meet the guy who ran CRAP, Jerome Winterton-Falle. It was surprisingly easy getting hold of him, something I wasn't expecting from a 'they're all listening' type of looney. A quick search of Twitter and their account came up. A quick direct message from me, and he called me almost instantly to arrange a meeting. First, I had to do research, and they'd been busy boys indeed.

He/they (had to get the correct pronouns) were members of the JAQ movement, which stood for 'Just Asking Questions'. The central pillar of this philosophy was a deep distrust of something the orange one used to quote a great deal, MSM or Mainstream Media. This actually struck a chord with me, not the political one but more of feeling they were all in it together, no matter which side of the fence they fell on politically. I was fed up with the main outlets, scaring the bejaysus of us. I gave up looking at the news unless for work. If they weren't telling us how bad the country or the world was at that present time (always worst in history), they gleefully told us how bad it would be in the future. If they didn't preach doom and gloom, people wouldn't need to watch, listen or read it. No one would tune into a bulletin that started with the headline 'All OK in the world. Best time in history ever. Nothing to see here!' However, where we veered away sharply were the reasons why the MSM was doing this. According to CRAP, various other groups and YouTube gurus with millions of disciples, they were part of a broader conspiracy of world elites. The aim of this higher echelon was to control and subjugate the masses for their own evil ends - power and money. To achieve their goals, lobotomising everyone by eliminating original human thought was essential. They said everything fed to us was controlled by these guys to create a narrative that suited their needs. So to the JAQ movement, the COVID vaccine and the effects of the disease was the perfect illusion created by those who were to benefit from doling it out to the masses.

Looking at CRAP's feed and site, plenty of those theories existed. They also wandered off into the territory I was most used to, the out-and-out plain looney. Many replies to their tweets used their moniker as an insult, JAQoffs being the most popular taunt. They'd also been a busy lot in protest- GM crops, 5G towers, etc. Usually dressed in bad fancy dress outfits that made a point, like a guy in a suit (one he wore to court the previous week) with a cigar to show he was a fat cat elite. He had a red substance all over their hands to signify having blood on their hands. They made sure other idiots were there to film their exploits and share them with the masses. There wasn't one political theme to it all, however. I was expecting an underlying anarchist or Marxist underbelly as there were with many environmental protest groups. Their ranks weren't made up of middle-class retirees and vicars, causing mayhem to the general public for a reason no one outside Surrey could fathom. They were made up from all walks of life and backgrounds, and all desired to not believe anything they were told by anyone.

I met him in an affluent part of London, Notting Hill, somewhere that was a living contradiction in urban sprawl. Ten million pound houses nestled beside crack dens. A bakery that would charge £20 for a coffee and croissant would be a few doors down from one of the roughest estates in London. The inhabitants of the nice houses were very wealthy, donated to good causes, diligently recycled, made sure their goods were ethical and allowed their children to run riot because they felt that giving them boundaries was a type of Nazi control. Then they'd jump in their Range Rovers and scoot down to Moreton-in-Marsh, where they charged even more for the coffee and croissant. That wouldn't matter because they knew a famous TV presenter or former PM.

I buzzed the button, which had a massive eye in the area generally reserved for the flat number. There was no 'hello' or 'who's this?' just a buzz, and the door opened. The hallway looked as though a bomb had gone off. Instead of carpet, the stairs were covered in flyers for pizza and curry, plus those envelopes that screamed bills. There was a reason why people didn't open bills; they looked so obviously like bills. If the company sending these out had put them in interesting-looking envelopes, they'd get way more opened. I suppose the opener would then be so angry they'd been duped they would then go and bomb the HQ of said energy company. I ascended a staircase with various bikes in the way, past a first-floor flat door that bore all the scars of being battered down by the police hammer in the past, to flat 3. The tell-tale sign of a dome above it indicating CCTV and a sign telling observers they were being watched. The door opened without me having to knock, and there stood before me was a man who, if people were asked to describe their archetypal hippie, this guy would be it. In a stained cream kaftan with Indian (I presumed) braiding around the edges, a long dark beard, long hair and a glint in his eye indicated he may have smoked something herbal a second before. The immediate smell of incense wafted from behind him. He was incredibly tall and had a self-confidence he could have borrowed from Edon. A handsome man, I was sure his ridiculous outfit never stopped him from going out with beautiful women. Guys like him just did, despite the laughter of mortals like me at the way they dressed. He lurched around the place like a sex pest with an ankle tag.

"How long had you known Lord Monaco?" I asked after refusing a hemp tea from a cup that had clearly been divorced from any type of washing liquid for some time.

"Oh, we met at a conference by Haven Mighty in Vegas." I googled him when I got back. He was the self-appointed, and everyone-else-appointed, leader of the JAQ movement worldwide.

"Not very good flying over to a conference in the USA whilst pretending to be an eco-warrior."

"I couldn't give a shit about the environment man. You're confusing me with someone else."

"Not what you're YouTube channel description says." I hadn't actually watched any of his videos though, so I formed my opinion purely on its title.

"It says I'm a warrior of the planet. It isn't the same."

"Sounds like it to me." He'd got me a bit riled up, which was only exasperated when a genuinely stunning woman appeared at the lounge door. Not ridiculously dressed but, as I had expected when I first saw him, she looked every inch a world-famous model and probably was. I had Bob at the back of my mind calling me a fuck'n numptie for not knowing the identity of the creature standing coquettishly in the doorway like an ancient Goddess. She asked him where the car key was and disappeared without looking my way.

"Being a warrior of the planet means not taking any shit from the people that control it. You and me are controlled man. Run our lives to suit their own nefarious needs."

"It's you and I."

"We're just raging against bullshit," he continued, oblivious to my grammar point. "We're exposing these fuckers for the lying, controlling bastards they really are." Jerome was a trustafarian. His father, grandfather and great-grandfather had made a fortune in the city, one of the main weapons the elite use to control us all, according to him. It was this wealth that allowed this particular guru dickhead to not work for a living, dressing it up as a crusade against the higher echelon. This cabal, of course, included his flesh and blood. One of the articles I found before our meeting said he and the dad were at war. Because they had nothing better to do, they'd turned vitriolic about each other and had gone their separate ways. Although Jerome still kept the pad in London, his trust fund was cut off, the poor soul.

"So you live like this despite them rather than because of them?"

"Exactly man. It's my mission in life."

"How lucky. You and the famous rock star just got on like best friends at this conference, right?"

"Yeah man, he was interested in our movement and what we were all doing. He wanted to set up a proper membership here and we were both going to do that together."

"But you needed money to do that."

"It helps."

"Vance's money."

"Hey, Vance wanted to use his money to expose this and advance our cause. Not for me to tell him how to spend it."

"Did you know he'd changed his will so that a nice fat chunk of cash was going to your organisation in the event of his death?"

"I didn't question the details. He had people for that. I just knew he was going to help." For the first time, he looked uncomfortable. This indicated he knew full well that as the sole director of the London chapter of the movement, he would be the beneficiary of a healthy sum.

"Did you get the money?"

"Surely you know more than me; the will is being contested." I couldn't help feeling that if the old boy told him he was back in the family, with all the trappings he would inherit as the eldest son, he'd give up the guru lifestyle, crack out the Hunters, tweed jacket and head down the M4 to run the estates. I started to gather my coat, bag and phone, rather wishing I'd see the girlfriend again. Even if she did make me feel ever-so inadequate, it was still worth seeing such beauty again.

"So you know about chemtrails right?" He asked.

"No."

"When you see a jet plane high in the sky leaving a trail from its wings, what do you think that is?"

"Never thought about it. They just do."

"They are trails of chemicals used to spray the world population."

"With what?"

"Question suppression."

"What the fuck's that?"

"They are chemicals man. Their properties are to suppress human thought so no one questions what those bastards are up to. It makes us all compliant to their control."

"You're in London, where thousands of planes fly overhead every day. So why haven't you, or me for that matter, been affected?"

"I'm getting negative vibes from you man." I realised that JAQ should actually stand for Just Allow Quiet!

11

Britney Amber was the Australian model who Lady Monaco wanted to rip her hair out. She was spectacularly beautiful, tall, tanned, blonde, and the camera truly loved her. As my gran used to say, she was 'all tits and teeth'. Before meeting Vance, she was just another stunning member of the profession. Although most of us don't usually mix with the beautiful people, they are there in their own cities or worlds. Anyone in fashion, music or movies will tell you that every single day, men and women who were extraordinarily lucky to have very good genes plied their trade. They used to go relatively unnoticed by the GP (general public) unless they reached a certain level of fame when the press and TV would gorge on their images and stories. With the advent of the internet and social media, any run-of-the-mill hot person could cook up a level of fame that enabled them to make a living. What really elevated any of these guys from the self-contained beauty bubble was to date someone famous. Then suddenly, things changed. Paps wanted to follow them, kids wanted their socials, and biz power players suddenly noticed. The rest of their career looked after themselves until an overdose or spectacular divorce. Pre-Vance, Britney had garnered a relative level of fame in the UK after appearing in something called the *Love Jungle*. Bob was suitably dismissive when I asked what that was. I wasn't a member of the ITV (It's Thick Vision) viewing family. That particular channel used to include GMTV (Get Moving Thickos Vision) which became GMB (Generally Moronic Britain). The broadcasters vying for the lowest common denominator competed in a race to the bottom. However, in the interests of research, I had to do something I'd have given my left testicle not to - watch a reality TV show.

The *Love Jungle* was billed as harmless fun, with singles doing horrible tasks in the jungle whilst trying to hook up with the other contestants. The whole series was available to stream, but I had to suspend the viewathon after the first one. It was the episode where Britney won the opening task. She had to fillet a fish as the chef for the evening, and her prize was a Sushi carving knife with a Japanese symbol on the end of the handle. Within each set of sexes, they all looked like each other. A few of the boys were making a good fist of crossing over into the girls though. I couldn't understand why people wanted to watch a load of Ken and Barbies with inane grins, skin like they slept in tea, badly acted histrionics, and a complete lack of insight into the world they live in. At the end of the ep, there was a discussion (if you can call it that) between two of the girls and two of the boys. As one of the girls said that she'd been really hurt by her last boyfriend, Britney said.

"I don't get hurt; I get even."

"You go, girlfriend," said the other tangoed girl. They all laughed, and a lad said, "I wish I could be more like you babe." According to Google, that guy turned out to win the thing with a girl (surprisingly) he declared his love for. One thing I could tell you, it was far from harmless. I'd seen something about how the broadcaster was rinsing stupid orange people around the country by flogging products related to the show. Also, I couldn't help thinking the drivel coming out of the contestants' mouths had a rotting effect on brain matter to the extent that anyone who listened to it immediately turned into a zombie incapable of original thought unless it was related to the show. Jerome came to mind.

I moved to Britney's insta profile, the main picture being her in a bikini. She had 100 thousand followers. Her bio stated:

Traveller, Lover, life sponge, MENSA member.

From what I'd seen, I doubted the MENSA bit. There were lots of pictures of her living the dream, or more accurately, the illusion of the dream. There was a promo for the jungle show where contestants were parachuting. What the consumers of that type of material didn't realise was 1) It was all mainly a sham & 2) the pressure on the content creator usually drove them mad. The sham bit was because no socials star ever rose to fame (or kept famous) by posting boring normal everyday occurrences. With so many of them out there and such a vast audience (all with attention spans of gnats), their posts had to be (delete where appropriate): inspiring/glamorous/thoughtful/amazing location/ sexy/blah blah. One picture can paint an entirely false image and not a representation of reality at all. But it racks up likes. Someone taking a selfie with the Sydney Opera House, the harbour and the blue skies behind them may just be wearing an ankle tab after their assault conviction. Simply running out of toilet roll and nipping down the corner shop didn't cut the mustard with any people who consumed the content. That led to number 2. Unlike the stars of old or non-socials stars, they had to perform all the time, had to provide content all the time and were under pressure to do so - all the time. That's not normal and can affect said creators' mental health, sometimes with awful consequences.

A post one week before Vance's death said:

Can't wait to catch you all at fluence con. I will have some huge news. Love you all. Be kind.

The last post stated:

It is with the deepest sadness that I have to announce the death of Vance Monaco. I'm so destroyed by this news like all his fans but also as his significant other. We'd been in a relationship and were going to announce it to all of you lovely people. I truly don't know how I will survive but will take strength from all your support. RIP Vance. Love you so much.

Cue the outpouring of sympathy with a lot of 'so sorry babes', 'sending totes love', the crying emoji, and various others used to express emotion lazily and generically. Some clearly didn't know what they were doing because there were thousands of likes and thumbs up.

The Hargreaves Exhibition Centre in Coventry was the venue for the fluence con. Apparently, the name was derived from Influencer. The centre is the only thing of any note in what was a massive toilet of an area. It was wet, grey, and filthy. A new burning car appeared every night, and there was an endless supply of shopping trolleys, which was strange because the nearest supermarket was ten miles away. I'd been there before for work when I attended a diet industry show; now that's another story. This show was all about social influencers. I struggled with that term, it being somewhat of a misnomer. Anyone with a hundred followers could call themselves an influencer. The fact their inane musings were only ever seen by their dog didn't seem to matter. There were huge crowds of smelly teenagers, many in bunches around various other teenagers sitting on high stools. It turned out the people perched on the stools were the grammers, YouTubers, and TikTokers. They were doing meet-and-greets and by the look on their faces, absolutely hated being in social contact with others less important than them. Their disciples didn't notice and were glued to their phones, taking photos, videos, and selfies. They asked utterly ridiculous questions and got suitably ridiculous answers.

I arranged to meet Britney in the centre's grandly titled *Press Office,* where we could talk in a quiet room with no one around. The press office at these things is usually a very drab room with a cripplingly bored person on the desk where you enter. They have to ask your name so you could receive your press badge, giving you unfettered access to all parts of the conference. There was some terrible coffee in a cheap flask and stale croissants on another table in the heart of the press operation. Depending on the exhibition, you got different types of journalists in this hub of activity. If it was an end-of-life one, they never covered anything exciting for the *Euthanasia Gazette,* so they were excited to have the badge to wear about the place; it made them feel important. If the exhibition was in something glamorous, such as the music industry, then the journos tended to hide their badges under say a jacket. If people didn't know who you were, it meant you were no one. Whilst I was waiting, one of the guys I recognised from the jungle show burst through the doors dramatically, clearly in a tiz. Behind him was a young guy in a suit with a very unimpressed look on his face.

"What the hell am I doing here?"

"They're paying you Giles," said the harassed lad following in Sir Prancelot's wake..

"Not enough."

"What's the problem? I'll see if I can fix it."

"Can you fix that the place is full of z-listers and wannabes? Make them famous so they can talk to me?"

"Of course, I'll get right on it." The lackey said sarcastically. Mr flouncy went silent. "Look, one pa left to do." He placed his hand on Giles' arm. "Then we're out of here, and I've booked lunch at the Gardonne." Giles pouted like a teenager but seemed cheered by the dinner venue reservation. Britney came in. Giles flew into completely OTT mode, all smiles, 'darlings' and air kisses. She replicated. They talked to each other as if on the west end stage, making sure they reached all the back areas of the theatre with their projection, even though it was just a press officer and me in there. Finally she made it over.

"Thanks for seeing me Ms Chalmers. I'm a little surprised you're here so soon after the tragic events."

"I feel I have to. To show strength for the sake of my fans. They've been amazing since I announced it."

"I'm sorry to kick off with this Ms Chalm..."

"Oh, call me Brit."

"Brit, what was Sir Vance's mental health situation before his death?"

"What do you mean?"

"Well, was he depressed, perhaps even not making sense?"

"He never made sense."

"And depression?"

"He didn't know the meaning of the word."

"So he wasn't acting strange?"

She looked at me questioningly, "When would I know strange?" That was the moment I binned the suicide theory.

"Ok, on to other things. What was the big news you mentioned in your Insta post before the accident?"

"I was going to announce our relationship to everyone and the fact that I was filming a new TV show." She picked up her phone and showed me a picture of Vance, not looking very happy, and Britney draped around him, laughing hysterically like it was a PR shoot. Also in the shot on either end were our friends, The Pilot and The Manager. They didn't look happy either

"I just can't believe that when I kissed him that night, it would be the last night I ever saw him." She sighed sadly, looking at the phone.

"And was he all on board with the whole TV show thing?"

"Of course, why wouldn't he be?"

"I'm sorry Ms Chalm...Brit, he just doesn't look that happy" She looked at the photo again.

"Ah, I suppose he doesn't. He'd just had an argument with Edon which is why he's scowling there."

"Oh, what were they arguing about?"

"Edon, who didn't like me by the way, wanted to sell Monnie's huge back catalogue of songs."

"And sir Vance, didn't want that?"

"No, he said that was his DNA. It was how people would remember him in generations to come. So he wanted to keep it as his."

"This might not have gone down well with Mr Thanisi?"

"No, it did not. He has a right temper on him, Colin, do you mind if I call you Colin?"

"Not at all..."

"He argued a lot with Monnie, who'd stopped trusting him. The beast even shouted at me many times, couldn't get over that my Vance had found love away from the ice maiden."

"When was that picture taken?"

"The party the night before he died. The crew were there to film it." Another moment of silence, looking at the phone, shaking her head, then a big breath. "I'm really sorry, but I have to move on to my next PA." And with that, she left as an assistant ushered her off to the next meet and greet. My dislike of reality stars had waned a bit as I was taken off guard by an open, warm, affable, and bright character.

On leaving the centre, a teenager bumped into me because he was looking down at the phone glued to his hand. He looked up in horror and shouted, "Get out of the bloody way Harry."

12

That morning began as usual as I opened up my e-mail account to 30 new messages. There was the usual spam, such as offers of pills to enlarge my penis. Hamjke, a Latvian girl, wanted to meet me because she was feeling sexy. A good Samaritan in Nigeria wanted to give me money; all I had to do was e-mail my bank details to him and I would be £500,000 richer. There were links to sites where I could see women enjoying sexual relations with farmyard animals and one that advertised a service in Holland that would help me end it all if I felt everything was getting too much. Only three e-mails were genuine. The first was from Sophie.

Hi All.

I'm throwing a surprise party for Hugh's birthday. It's on Saturday 30th May at 3 p.m. It is a surprise so if you can't make it by 3 p.m., please go round the block or something until we do the deed on Hugh. We don't want to blow the whole thing. And it goes without saying not to mention a word of it to Hugh, doesn't it, Colin?

Hope you can all make it.

Love,

Sophie

Sophie mentioned me in particular because of my reputation for leaking like a sieve. Throughout my life, people had always opened up to me. I didn't know whether it was because I was a good listener (whatever that meant) or I just had the ability to put people at ease. I never really analysed why, but drink was usually a factor. These nuggets of information never materialised after large amounts of water had been consumed. I'd lost count of the number of people who'd told me they were cheating on their partners or who had revealed sexual proclivities that were best kept to themselves. Take Geoff, for example. He was a uni pal, and we worked together when temping and did the same shitty jobs as me. He moved into banking when I joined the police. Suzie was his long-term girlfriend from school (ahhh). They lived together in his flat, and it looked like a dead cert that they would get married one day.

"Listen, if I tell you something, you can't tell anyone else," he dropped in the conversation while we were drinking in a Greenwich pub. That location is pertinent because we were there interviewing river taxi passengers for a survey by the Port of London Authority. After a few attempts to accost said passengers, we soon made the discovery that these guys would have rather jumped in the river than talked to us about their experience on it. So we went off to the pub where our creativity in making up answers would be considerably enhanced by beer.

"Of course. No one, your secret is safe with me. What is it?" I said with conviction.

"No really. This is serious and you must swear not to tell anyone."

"Totally. I promise." I was flattered Geoff trusted me with whatever he was about to tell me. But, of course, I never intended to reveal it.

"It's very embarrassing and ruining my life." I thought the smell of terminal illness was in the air. He'd said it was embarrassing, so I reckoned on testicular cancer.

"OK. What is it?"

"I'm addicted to wanking."

"What?" I spluttered into my beer.

"I'm addicted to it. Can't stop. I'm doing it over 30 times a day." My desire to scream in laughter had to be held back when I saw how severe Geoff's face was. It most definitely was embarrassing – and utterly ridiculous. Why was he telling me this? "No, this is serious. I have to do it twice before I go to work. Then at work, I have the urge the whole time. I have to go to the toilet and use video clips on my phone as inspiration. I rush home from work to beat Suzi back to the flat so that I can have a couple before her arrival." I screamed inside for him to stop talking before I died of internal injuries from holding in the laughter. He stayed silent long enough for me to compose myself and ask a question.

"What about Suzi?"

"Of course she doesn't know."

"I meant she's your girlfriend, and you have sexual urges. Doesn't she satisfy them?"

"Oh yeah, if it wasn't for her I'd be doing double that amount.

It's just never enough. I don't know what's wrong, so I'm going to America for help. They have a therapy regime over there for people suffering from the same condition." What can you say to that? The image of an American self-help group for sufferers was too much to resist.

"Is it like AA where you get up, introduce yourself and state that you are a wanker, at which stage they all give you a one-handed clap, the other one being busy, of course?"

"That's just bloody rude and insensitive. You're taking the piss out of my very serious condition. You'd better not tell anyone. I couldn't handle the embarrassment," he said and then moved the conversation on. The topic was closed.

Despite my original intentions, I e-mailed my friend in the City at the first opportunity. The City had always been the source of the sickest jokes. They managed to get them into circulation so quickly, particularly after a disaster. I put the whole conversation down in the e-mail, and the return mail just said what an amazing story it was. I thought nothing more of it. The next day, I was alerted to a report on one of the news sites entitled 'I'm addicted to pulling my pud.' It turned out that my e-mail had done the rounds in the square mile and then the rest of London, eventually finding its way to the newspaper. If that wasn't bad enough, I had included Geoff's name in the e-mail, which had been duly printed. A week later, there were entries on TikTok in which people had done spoof videos set to music. One particular one was set to Queen's *Bohemian Rhapsody* with lines like 'Thunderbolts and wanking, very very frightening.' Needless to say, Geoff or Suzie never spoke to me again, but he did get the therapy that worked, and they married and had children.

Emails done; it was time for a walk. I was full of the joys of late summer. Unbelievably for the U.K., there was a clear blue sky, the one that lifted the soul and filled you with hope and positivity. This was particularly true after spending summer under the usual grey cotton wool blanket in the sky that sapped the soul and made you think why we lived in this damn country. I was pleased but puzzled by Lady M's appearance in the shithole of *The Oak*. As I rounded the corner out of smell range of Tommy, a people carrier pulled up at speed and then screeched to a halt making the tyres smoke. It was like something out of *Bourne*. To continue that theme, a few brick shithouses jumped out, all with no hair or very short haircuts, wearing black fatigue combats and black tshirts. They possessed the sort of aura of menace you really would only find in a Russian gulag. The bald man-mountain I found myself in front of had clearly really practiced the look. He gave the impression he'd eat my children if I had them. Although he was the same height as me, he was immense crossways. His shoulder was as big as my whole upper torso. He moved up to my face without an effortless glide, never associated with such a massive unit.

"We want you to come with us." said the tank. My immediate instinct was to run. Most self-defence experts worth their salt will not teach you not how to fight an attacker. They will teach you how to land something that buys you time to run away. That's what my SAS mate told me. Why risk a fight when you can get away from the confrontation and the possibility of being filleted by a sushi chef. So off I went in the direction away from the interlopers. I hadn't noticed the dauschaund that had wandered into my vicinity, the owner not far behind. The lead and then the dog got under my feet, the latter issuing a yelp of pain as I fell on it. The next thing I remember is becoming conscious that I was awake, with an unbelievable headache.

"Fuck, I've gone blind!" I shouted. I was aware of being awake but couldn't see anything but black.

"No, you just have a blindfold on idiot," said an Eastern European accent close to my ear. I recognised his voice being the Drax-looking guy with the muscles. I was utterly confused now. Searing headache, blind and some villain (I assumed) from a spy movie telling me to shut it and calling me an idiot. "We are here to tell you to drop the case. We have interests that feel you will seriously be compromised with your investigation." The pain took over my whole brain, so I went for a stock avoidance technique.

"But the police would do the same," I offered. There was an extended and exaggerated laugh from all the occupants.

"Yeah right, the police," said the leading voice and laughed loudly again, followed by the others. The guy scaring the shit out of me was clearly the boss.

"Listen," his voice hushed, sounding as though he's moved a lot closer. "I know you have no family of your own, but what about your father?" This was a bit of a shock. In all my time in the police and my new-found role as a PI, my father had never entered into the equation. He lived on the Spanish Costa Del Sol (or Costa Del Crime, he would always like to joke with me when I was plod) and had done since my mother died. So when she passed, he thought why should he live in this country with: 'Pissing rain all the time. Grey skies, all the time. Rude, angry people.' I didn't want to tell him that all countries have those. The list wasn't small of things he didn't like about the UK, so he sold the house and bought a small 2-bed villa in Almeria. This was a jolt to me. Then came a smell I recognised as a Bubbles special. Suddenly the occupants erupted in a speedy and animated native tongue that sounded from Eastern Europe or Russia. I got the gist from their unguessable language that they were unhappy with someone called Alexi. A breeze rushed through as I heard all the windows go down, and they returned to English.

"Fuck me Alexi." As the air circulated, I wondered if Alexi would take Bubbles in, they'd be perfect together. Then, after a minute or so of guys going 'phew', I felt a hand on my forearm.

"Think about it, Mr Todd. I strongly suggest you give this one, how you say, a wide berth."

"Like Alexei," said another voice with laughter ensuing from the goons, but they quickly and immediately silenced. Then the leading voice came right to my ear. "Fuck off and leave it all alone. Now. Understand?" Then the sound of a sliding door opening, and I felt a searing pain again, this time on my shoulder as I was thrown out of the, thankfully stationary, people carrier.

I called the police when I got up. I thought there might be a chance that they'd rush to my aid. It was after a kidnapping, a serious offence, and even might even have had the possibility of nabbing the bastards that did it; the van would still be in the area. They took fifteen minutes to get to me. By then, the *Bourne* lot had well and truly scarpered. The officers did try to call in CCTV footage, but the van had disappeared. I never had problems with London becoming one of the most CCTV-ridden cities in the world outside China. That was as long as it was there to protect citizens or at least be able to track down criminals. If you were a crim, you'd get captured on CCTV. If you weren't, then so what? I didn't put any store in the claims from civil liberties groups, human rights worriers or people like Jerome. They said that The State would use them to control us and subject them to dictatorial control. However, there was a camera-related issue that sent my blood pressure spiralling through the roof. That was when they were used to tax people for entering a city under the guise of saving the environment. These sprung up all over the country as councils realised they could fleece citizens in what was supposed to be a good cause. They were just revenue creators for cash-strapped local authorities. The act of piracy and restriction of movement by a body on the public didn't have political party affiliations. They were all at it. London was the originator of these heinous intrusions into daily lives and the architect of ULEZ (Ultra Low Emission Zone). It got a little grey when talking speed cameras though. The police claimed they were there to catch people breaking the law. Which they were, exceeding the speed limit. Speeding was classed as an offence, and police said speed limits help keep people safe. There were different limits depending on the type of road and the type of vehicle. However, when returning to those little dictator-complex councils, I got a little unsure. In the 'interests of safety and the environment,' they lowered the speed limits to ridiculous, impractical limits. They then installed cameras to catch unsuspecting drivers unaware of the change. My theory was, again, they were just making a cash grab. Anyway, back to the kidnappers, despite there being relatively good camera coverage in the area, the guys knew what they were doing. The plates were cloned and knew the network's blackspots, and after being caught after throwing me out, they disappeared after that. Finding out about these guys had Bob written all over it. That was his world.

13

I waited for Matty at Euston Station. He was a very old friend visiting London from somewhere up north. I never knew exactly where he lived because, like all southern dickheads, I really didn't have a clue about the geography of most of the North. I knew where the cities were of course – Manchester, Liverpool, Glasgow, Edinburgh etc. But give me a town name, and I'm stumped. I met, liked and loved many northerners but when they told me the town of the village they were from, they might as well have been explaining a little-known star in the outer universe. The usual reaction to my ignorance was either a) an understanding that they'd get this down south all the time and reference it to distance from one of the main cities, or b) take umbrage that the world didn't know a place that was dear to their hearts.

Matty was someone I'd known since primary school when we used to charge at each other in games of British Bulldog at lunchtime. To be fair though, he didn't actually do much charging because he was a slightly tubby child. Matty was always the one who got tagged first because, like a pack of lions going for the weak prey, the guys in the middle would catch him before even leaving the starting line. His parents always claimed that he was big-boned, but we all knew that wasn't quite right even at that young age. Unfortunately for him, the puppy fat didn't disappear as the years passed. He got all the usual abuse at secondary school and started getting larger as he got older. When he went on to university, discovering the student lifestyle meant his weight problem went nuclear. The culture of binge drinking, takeaway and very little exercise meant he ballooned from a fat kid to an immense young adult. His diet was atrocious. I remember going up to see him for a weekend and wondering how any human could survive what he was stuffing down his throat. His average day's consumption started with three bacon sandwiches for breakfast. Elevenses consisted of two Cornish pasties. There was a huge burger and chips for lunch and copious packets of crisps and chocolate bars before dinner. The Indian takeaway that specialised in inedible meat kormas usually provided his dinner out of a carton. All this was washed down with up to fifteen pints of bitter. He was a heart attack waiting to happen.

There was a fat-related incident in freshers' week which made him a legendary and popular campus figure, very unlike the experience of being hounded at school. This week was when all the kids who'd never been away from home on their own tried to get used to being free from the apron strings. It was a time when friendships were made that would last the duration of the course and beyond. It was also a seminal week for Matty. He returned to the residents' halls at 3 a.m. after a night on the lash with his fellow inmates. He was making them all laugh with a rant about his shower being too small and unable to fit into it. Keen to keep his audience laughing, he ushered them into his bedroom to illustrate the point with a practical demonstration. Still fully dressed, he faced the shower and got everyone to push behind him to squeeze him in.

'You see? You see?' he shouted with his back still to the crowd because there was no room to turn around. Everyone's laughter was interrupted by a loud crack. When they discovered the noise came from the shower floor that was giving way under Matty's considerable weight, the laughter turned to mass hysterics. There were two other cracks, and then the floor suddenly gave way totally. He ended up wedged in the space where there used to be a floor, like a marshmallow stuffed into a thimble. There were a few half-hearted attempts to pull him out by the arms, but it was soon apparent that he was well and truly stuck. The general consensus was that the situation could only be resolved by the fire brigade. Two engines arrived, and the firefighters spent a good amount of time openly laughing at Matty before beginning to tackle the problem at hand. Matty's predicament caused a crowd to gather along the hallways and in front of the building entrance. Messages went pinging around the campus, which resulted in a good two hundred drunken students all jeering and waiting for Matty to emerge. The firefighters first used the circular saw to cut the floor around him so they could get access to whatever was trapping his leg and pull him out. Then, they used ropes around his waist and three men on each arm to extract him. The collective heave onto the bathroom floor was accompanied by Matty's deafening scream of agony as his leg was broken halfway between his knee and foot.

Now they were faced with a dilemma. The ambulance stretcher would not take his weight without crumpling like paper, and there was no other way to carry him out. Matty would have to hop out with the support of the firefighters. It took them almost an hour to work Matty down to the lobby because they had to stop for the paramedics to give him more gas and adjust his splint. When they finally emerged from the front door, a huge cheer went up from the waiting mob. The footage recorded on phones of him stuck, and the subsequent rescue made him an instant socials worldwide hit. The student paper took an altogether PC tack. It blamed the university for scrimping the money when building the residence halls. They started a campaign to accept overweight people as a recognised minority who should be given all the rights other groups like disabled people were afforded. They wanted the university to spend money reinforcing anything that might give way under a large person, such as shower rooms, toilets, beds and canteen chairs. They used Matty as the campaign spearhead, something he was very unhappy about. He didn't want to be the spokesman for anything. He came to college to have fun, and getting involved in that sort of nonsense was not his idea of a laugh. However, all the publicity made him a cult figure. It meant that he spent the duration of his stay at the university as the most famous person on campus. After he left college, he managed to get a job in a marketing agency in Manchester. Actually working for a living meant he lost weight. Although no longer medically obese, he was no racing snake, that was for sure. He was a popular figure around the office and made friends quickly. We always had fun when we got together.

I watched a flock of rats with wings (pigeons) eating some kebab someone had dropped on the station concourse. They were the ugliest bunch of avians I'd ever seen. Many of them had stumps instead of feet. I wondered if they had set up their nest on the electrified tube lines, meaning they lost a foot every time they stepped on it. The phone went, it was Bob.

"So what did you find out about his crew?" I asked.

"Did you just say crew?" His intonation suggested that people who weren't dragging their knuckles on the ground should avoid criminal colloquies. He always forgot that I'd been locking the scumbags up for quite a few years before my private enterprise.

"Just tell me about them."

"The big thing about Albanians is they live on their rep. Much like them South American nuttas hang'n people from bridges and chopping heads off. They like to have people think they'd cut your Alberts (*Albert Hall – Ball*) off for just looking at them.

"They didn't seem that bad or surely they would have really done me in."

"Trust me porot, you don't wanna mess with these lot, I tell ya. One of their gang had their motor stolen and his dog was shot in the robbery right. So this geezer what lost the car and the dog, then murdered the whole lot of the robbers out of revenge."

"That's John Wick."

"Nah, straight up."

"And where does Thanisi fit it?"

"Word is, when he came back here, he'd gone native. But there was something about a debt, a debt he owed them. These aren't the sort of people you want to owe a debt to."

"I'm still looking at the idea Monaco topped himself."

"No chance. He was a rock god. Played to millions of people all over the world for over forty years. There aint nothing he aint done, no one he aint shagged, played with or met. He shat gold ringos (*cockney rhyming translation - Ringo Star - bar*) and then when nearly a bloody pensioner, he meets a new fit bird more than half his age. Why on God's green would he wanna top himself?" Bob did have a point.

Matty and I watched a man argue with his wife in a restaurant.

"You're the one who fucking saw my best man without telling me," hubby spat.

"He is in a bad place at the moment. He just wanted to talk."

"So why not tell me?"

"He didn't want me to. He felt embarrassed and couldn't talk to you about it."

"You fucked him didn't you?"

"Of course not. Why don't you trust me."

"Because you kept meeting him from me which makes me suspicious."

"You're an idiot," she said, threw her wine over him and stormed out. The whole restaurant was silent, staring at the now lone diner at table 13. There were several ways he could have fronted out being such a bellend. I personally would have loudly exclaimed, 'I don't think anyone noticed that did you?' and sipped my wine. Instead, after all the commotion, we started talking about the case. Matty loved investigating stuff. He was one of those internet warriors who would research what politicians, celebrities, pundits, and the rest, said to fact-check and expose any irregularities. He had a Twitter account with 3 million followers. The nonsense spotted by the great and the good was present in almost everything anyone ever said. He knew I was on the case and had been doing research, something I possibly should've been doing.

"Have you looked at Companies House?" he asked.

"It was next on the list."

"Your pilot was the MD of the Flying Aces."

"No shit Sherlock." The man with wine all over him got up and left with as much dignity as he could muster. There was no going back for him with the diners though.

"But did you know that Monaco was the only shareholder?" Matty said, knowing the answer would be no. Now this was news. What if Vance found out about the drug runs? How would that have played out with the two of them?

14

It was time for the event of the month - karaoke night in the *Oak & Saw.* I would usually have had broken bamboo shoved under my fingernails than go to such a prestigious event. The last one resulted in the boys in blue being called after it was attended by a group of youths celebrating one of their lot being released from prison. They were well-known hoodlums with short fuses who couldn't handle their drink. After several attempts to take over the karaoke machine and throw off regulars, they kicked off. The regulars were a group of ordinary kids just having a laugh, and punches were thrown in the resulting fracas. Sequins had to step in to calm it down and help Roger kick them out. That was accompanied by the usual threatening blah blah 'we're gonna get you fucker' 'you're fucking dead,' etc. Once outside, they didn't disperse, generally making a nuisance of themselves. When a disabled parking road sign came through the window, it was time to call the police. Turned out a couple of them were on parole and were returned to the embrace of the prison system. So their rendition of the *Beastie Boys, No Sleep Till Brooklyn* had particular resonance. Their jail was in Brooklyn, North Yorkshire.

How did I end up going to this one? Bob had something for me. I questioned why he couldn't email it, talk about it over the phone, or even zoom in. He was in the pub, and I needed to see him sharpish. He didn't trust email or even the phone for imparting sensitive information or, more accurately, telling me stuff that could get his associates in trouble. This deep suspicion of electronic communication was ingrained in him from an early age, as his descendants had. After all, cockney slang was invented by Victorian criminals as a way to talk to each other about stuff, usually robbery, doing someone in and such like, without the police understanding a word of what they were talking about. However, despite his nickname, whenever I asked him to find stuff out for me, he usually came back with something I could use.

We watched as Geraldine and Donald took to the stage to absolutely murder 'Save your love' that inducing duo for Renee and Renata from the 80s. The one with the video where he constantly looked as though he was struggling to hold in a number 2, and she looked like she was waiting for the crooner opposite her to croak.   There was a moment where the two lovebirds (not Renee and Renate but Geraldine and Donald) looked lovingly into each other's eyes as they sang the chorus. Because hubby's gaze was concentrated on his good lady wife and not used to performing on a stage, he lost underfoot awareness. He lifted his left foot and went to take a step towards his co-crooner. Instead of a solid stage, he stepped into thin air beyond the stage edge. He disappeared without drama, like a sack of spuds being chucked off a cliff. As everyone gasped, and silence reigned, he bounced his enormous frame straight up from the floor shouting 'Who put that fucking step there?' It was worth the £5 admission fee alone. That was a natural break point for the singing.

"The pilot's broke, according to a few blokes I know," Bob told me. I never wanted to know who these blokes were, nor them me. Bob's background was best described as colourful. He was from a family of 8 kids (five brothers and 3 sisters). According to Bob, his father was a very virulent man. He supposedly just had to look at a woman to make them pregnant, so the mum would 'get a bun in the oven' at the drop of a hat. I questioned the usefulness of such prowess when the old man was serving 15 years for armed robbery but no, he also got four female prison guards pregnant when banged up. So with the fatherly figure in the household absent without leave and a little remiss in standard moral guidance anyway, the boys also drifted into erring on the wrong side of the law. All had been arrested for petty theft, drug offences and anti-social behaviour. ASBOS were handed out like sweets amongst them all. A couple graduated to the more serious stuff like car theft and firearm possession, with both doing stints at her (then) majesty's pleasure. Bob started driving for a local gangster and so stopped actually doing the crimes, just driving the bloke around who controlled the criminals. He liked the job, it wasn't taxing and he got out and about. He was paid very well but didn't have to do anything bad to do. He was clean. The boss had known his father and felt a sense of duty towards Bob, so he ensured he wasn't ever told anything about the gangs' activities. When his father was released early on good behaviour, he and the boss did a bank job straight after and both were caught when the ink in the money bags exploded all over them. Now both doing porridge, Bob moved into driving celebrities and hedge fund managers who were 'Just as bent as the gangsters'. However, his family, friends, and their family and friends were all involved somehow in criminal activity in some way or other. I would have been as welcome as a sausage at a bar mitzvah if any of these guys were to have a gathering and I turned up.

"Brilliant information Bob, well worth the money. I can end my investigation right now."

"Fuck you very much."

"Well, I'm hoping there's more."

"Alright smart arse, you wanna hear?"

"Fire away."

"He likes a flutter like DiCaprio likes a Victoria's Secret model, if you know what I mean." I didn't. "In fact, it had taken his house and he was well and truly in the shit."

"So?"

"So, to make up moolah, he was using his planes to drop loads other than skydivers."

"What sort of loads?"

"Drugs prof." Because Bob knew I had a degree, he thought I was academically bright. He didn't know that the qualification was in classics, a degree subject - in which Bubbles could have got a 2:1 in. I still never corrected him on this though. He'd found out that Clause would book skydiving trips in Spain for UK Flying Aces punters. These customers met him at the jump site in San Hepatalon, where he'd brought the plane from the UK.

They'd have a weekend of it, and then when everyone else flew back normally, the pilot would return in the jump plane, this time carrying tonnes of cocaine loaded on at the site. When he got to a remote part of the New Forest, he dumped his payload out the back to be picked up by the buyers. All was legit in the eyes of the authorities. Because Clause was an expert at dropping parachutes onto a dime from high up, no one on the ground ever saw anything suspicious.

As Roids started a truly terrible rendition of 'My Way', Bob had more info for me.

"So I know this geezer who's a brass handler."

"A what?"

"A guy who looks after the brasses (*doesn't have any rhyming slang but just means prostitute*) he's straight up a top bloke by the way." Knowing BB, I doubted this glowing testimony. "Well our boy Vance was a bit of a regular with some of the girls."

"How come that never got in the press?"

"He's not as stupid as a footballer. Anyway, he liked all sorts of stuff that'd make your jaw drop. Real kinky shit man."

"A bit of the abnormal eh?"

"When you can have anything you want and have had it done for 20 or 30 years, normal gets a bit fucked."

"What if he was going to be exposed for this?"

"Trust me, that was never going to happen. Mani wouldn't allow it." Mani was the nice guy looking after the prostitutes. His name was derived from a manicure on account of his penchant for removing fingernails of people who needed sorting. "I tell you what though, he was back at it with the wife." Even though they had separated, and Monaco was living with Britney, Sir and Lady would go to orgies, swinging, and fetish clubs together. Their voracious and eclectic sexual appetite as a couple had been legendary for decades and they were continuing that on despite their separation.

"So what has all this, agreed interesting, information got to do with the case?"

"You're the detective, you tell me." Thankfully, the Karaoke machine blew a fuse leaving an excellent silent hole where musical torture had been before. "How'd it go with Bambi?" he asked me, referring to my last date - or nearly date. For those of you not on the dating scene, there were a million dating apps bringing all sorts of lonely, horny, and crazy souls together. The principal is pretty much the same with all of them, no matter how much they try to dress up why they are different to the others. They all boil down to people creating profiles and uploading a set of photos. Then you're shown all the pictures in the dating criteria range you're interested in. It's just a matter of swiping left on the image if you don't like them and right if you do. If that person has done the same, then you match and can chat. The one I used allowed people to send a like to the person before swiping, thus making contact before the match. This was a little disheartening as the only ones that ever sent a like were either too young or too old. No one in my age preference ever sent me a like. The grannie likes were deleted straight away. The youngens made me pause when I first saw them as they were usually very beautiful and in some state of skimpiness. But after a 'wow', they too were dispatched for being young enough to be my daughter. The other thing with the younger variety, sending a like to someone so much older than them, usually indicated they were after something akin to a sugar daddy. I was still unsure of the whole sugar phenomenon. To me, it just sounded like prostitution, where the guy pays for the company of a beautiful young girl. Although it's supposedly not expressed in all my research, I can guarantee the guy paying for the privilege was expecting sex in return. The people involved often referred to it as a relationship. I showed one of these to Bob once. A stunning girl who listed her interests as 'fine dining, being spoilt, travel, etc.' Some photos wouldn't be out of place in Vogue as she supped champagne in various fancy restaurants. The images also included shots of worldwide landmarks in the background. The one of her in a bikini, looking out from a plunge pool overlooking a safari scene with giraffes in the background, made Bob proffer his considerable dating knowledge.

"Fuck me. Check that out. You should take her out."

"You don't get it Bob. She's looking for money. Why else would she like someone my age?"

"But if you do go out with her, then the joke's on her coz you got fuck all, but she may think you do."

"She'll smell a rat, trust me." However, I thought about it for several days and started texting her. She seemed really nice and normal. We had a phone call that lasted half an hour with plenty of laughter. Maybe I was wrong, and so went for the plunge on the following text.

Me: So we should go out on a date sometime?

Her: I'd love that baby. That made me sit up a bit, calling me baby so early on.

Me: Ok, how about we meet for coffee on Thursday?

Her: What?

Me: A coffee. Silence ensued so I backed up the offer. *Me: It's not so formal as a date. If we get on, we get on and can then go to dinner.*

Her: Did you read my profile?

Me: Of course.

Her: It very clearly says fine dining. I don't do coffee dates.

Me: Oh, why not? I was immediately blocked and felt foolish for thinking otherwise.

Bob had a habit of getting names ever so very slightly wrong. Everyone knew who he was talking about but it was usually a case of close but no cigar. When I told him about this exchange, he showed this capability to the full.

"Casserova strikes again!"

15

It was time to have a look at the house Monaco shared with Britney and the place he departed from on that fateful morning. I arranged details with Ms Savagae, who emailed me the address in Warwickshire and instructions for the gate entry code and various alarms. She said no-one would be there for at least a couple of weeks. I probably should have started with this task at the beginning of the case, but due to misdirected priorities, I was late to the party.

After a trek from the train station in the horizontal rain (the location was way too far for the scooter) and having finally found the address, I tried to read the access code printed with the instructions. The weather made it hard for me to see the email on my phone; I'd reached the age where trouble was had with reading small print. I entered the code expecting the iron gates to part like the red sea for Moses, but nothing happened. I tried again and again with the same result. I hadn't noticed or heard an electric private security smart car roll up behind me.

"Can I help you sir?" boomed a voice from the patrol vehicle that made me jump, spilling the phone onto the pavement. This was the type of security where wealthy neighbours cubbed together to fund patrols as they were sick of waiting three days for a copper to come round after they had been burgled.

"Oh brilliant, thank you," I said as I scrambled for my

phone. He got out of the car, a hairy bear dressed as a security guard for a fancy dress party. He got closer.

"Sir, do you know the people in there?"

"Oh yes, well sort of. I'm a private investigator looking into he murder of Sir Vance Monaco. This has all been arranged with Ms Savage." Brian Blessed started talking into his radio. Although he had no powers of arrest, he could make life a right pain for me. I just wanted this over quickly without answering a lot of questions. I gave the code one more go, this time with a hashtag on the end that I'd missed previously. Voila! The gates started opening.

"Really should bring my glasses." I said to a still suspicious bear.

The front of the house was imposing in real life. A Georgian mansion that dated back all of ten years. It did, however, illustrate the cornerstones of Georgian architecture - square, made of brick, symmetrical windows and a Grand entrance embellished with arches and columns.

After looking around many marbled rooms bigger than my flat, I went up the vast sweeping staircase. I was still unsure what I was looking for, but I persevered. The main bedroom was a homage to the 80s when Thunderbolt finally made it into the big time. The Warhol and a couple of Hockneys on the walls had to be real. A lava lamp stood on a plinth at the foot of the bed in front of the grand wall-to-wall mirrored wardrobe. For some reason, I decided to open it. As the internal cupboard lights came on, they revealed Britney standing there. She promptly screamed, which scared the bejaysus out of me. I stumbled backwards and kicked the lava lamp stand, which sent the light backwards. It hit the wooden bedpost, smashed and deposited the fluorescent blue liquid all over the white bed and cream carpet. I stared in shock at the unholy mess, then at an equally shocked Britney.

We gathered our thoughts in the kitchen. I found a half-empty bottle of Yamazaki, one of the first Japanese single malt whiskeys to make it here and as much a superstar as Monaco was. We both needed it for medicinal purposes.

"That lamp, the mess," I said into the cut glass tumbler.

"That was one of the things he gave me."

"Oh God, I'm sorry. Was it really expensive?"

"Don't think so. It was a prize he'd won at a fair when a kid and kept it all these years." Having heard that, I knew I'd still be paying the value back from my grave.

"I suppose you're wondering why I'm hiding in the closet here?"

"It has crossed my mind."

"I wanted to get some personal items." She gestured at the box in front of her on the kitchen counter.

"Why couldn't you do that before?"

"I've not been allowed to come here since his death. Lady Monaco took over and changed the access codes. But, I'm sure you've found out, I wasn't exactly on her Christmas card list."

"How'd you get in?"

"I get on very well with the housekeeper. I was the only one who spoke to her like a person, not an employee." I started lifting the box lids up to look inside. They were quickly closed by

Britney.

"I'm sorry, these are personal items. Sentimental value."

"I'd love to have a look, just in case there's anything that might help me." Unfortunately, I couldn't demand to see what was in the box.

"There are some very private and embarrassing things, you know, of a sexual nature." She said apologetically. Knowing what a dirty bugger he was, I certainly didn't want to see Monaco's sex toys, so I left the matter.

"Yu know, Vance was convinced people were out to get him," she said, sipping her whiskey.

"I've heard 'fucking nuts' been mentioned a few times" Not my finest moment.

"He'd found out stuff about his supposed friends that just made him more paranoid. He felt he couldn't trust anyone but me."

"One final question, if that's OK Brit?"

"Shoot."

"Are you really a member of MENSA?" She smiled a cabin crew smile. That profession had perfected the art of being polite and professional, no matter how much they wanted to stick burning needles in the eyes of the rude, demanding passenger.

"Yes Colin, I am."

16

Back to my first encounter with Britney. She'd given me quite a big piece of news. There was a party on the night before Vance's death at his home. My chief persons of interest so far, the manager and the pilot, were there. This satisfied the two main criteria of the crime. I'd discovered that this house was the site of the parachute room where Vance stored all his kit, including the stuff he would use on the day of his final jump. It would have been easily accessible to all partygoers. Both Thanisi and Walner were experts and would have known precisely where to cut the risers so that Vance didn't see them until it was too late. They could have done it that night whilst all present were off their heads. Vance would have picked up the parachute in the morning none the wiser. Also, Thanisi's motive had shown itself in numerous forms: revenge for his sister's treatment and wanting to sell Vance's back catalogue but not being allowed. These two needed another talking to.

The producers of the TV show provisionally called *At Home With The Monacos* had been very helpful and enlightened me on making TV for people with a penchant for hair extensions, vodka Red Bull and doughnuts. They explained that as a subject of a reality programme, if you sat down on the back of a superyacht in the med, of course, you'd feel fantastic as the sitee. But just staring out at the beautiful turquoise sea makes for truly terrible TV unless said subject falls off the back and is attacked by a Great White. It's why even the most real of supposed reality TV is very carefully planned. Were it not, the program makers would just sit around watching the idiots itching their butts like monkeys in a cage. If you've ever seen animals at the zoo, that's pretty much all they do. That could, of course, be because they're in a cage rather than the jungle.

I was given all the footage that had been shot at the party, apparently called 'the rushes' a name whose origin goes back to the days when TV presenters wore dinner jackets and spoke like King George VI. The much-needed bottle of claret, cigarettes, and a clean ashtray was set up. The difference between these rough shots and an edited complete programme showed what a job they did after the cameras had been put down. Immediately the terribly shaky camera annoyed me. The producers told me it was all the rage in TV and everyone was doing it and added authenticity. It just added nausea and a sense that someone had accidentally filmed it, the TV equivalent of a pocket dial. It took an hour of nonsense to finally get to something interesting. Vance was being interviewed in the parachute room, the line of packs behind him. Whist the cameraman was going through various settings on his equipment, he was still recording it. In the old days of tape being used to record footage, it was expensive to video unless you were absolutely ready and sure about your shot. With the advent of digital technology in cameras, that need disappeared. A memory card was the cost of a pint and could record ten times more footage than a tape. So the crew would start the recording while fine-tweaking lighting, sound etc. Whilst this went on, Vance broke off, went halfway down the line of chutes and measured in his mind using his hands up against his eyes, like a painter, for perspective. He then moved the parachute a millimetre and returned to his interview position in front of the lens. He was asked if he was ok by a voice behind the camera.

"I'm just a bit OCD," he replied.

"OK, So just start with 'this is my parachute room.' and go from there," the voice said.

"OK."

"What's the wifi code?" came another voice off camera.

"There's no wifi and make sure your Bluetooth is off or this ain't going anywhere. They are the devil's work." Then, someone else from the crew told everyone to check their phones.

"When I ask you a question, give it a couple of seconds before you answer to help in our edit," continued the first voice. Vance shot a scolded look as though the crew member had said his music was naff and he was too old to wear those clothes. Then they were rolling.

"What goes on here Vance?"

"It's where my kit is put together and checked the day before a jump."

"And who checks it?" He waited the few seconds.

"Depends who's here and who's jumping with me."

"And tell us what Skydiving means to you."

"Apart from music, it's my greatest love. We call it skyfalling as your mind goes totally blank and your worries completely disappear. You're hurtling towards the ground at two hundred miles an hour - free as a bird." A mischievous glint appeared in his eye. "You can't think of any fucking thing else because it's noisy as fuck, like a train fucking your ears. Then there's someone constantly kicking you in the balls as you fall to earth." Vance waited a couple seconds as instructed previously. "You can't use that right!" and started laughing hysterically. Someone who'd been in the business as long as he knew more about directing and filming interviews than any of the crew at his house that night.

"Let's go again," said the voice.

The next shot of interest I stumbled upon featured Britney. She was at the corner of the vast open-plan entertaining space with the party thronging behind her. There was the air of the cat that got the cream, flashing those insanely white teeth and throwing her hair back as she set up for her piece on camera. Holding a glass of fizz (I suspected Prosecco, she didn't strike me as in the same socio-economic group grouping as Lady M). A tray of canapes carried by a waiter floated by. I once read an article by a hilarious food writer about catered canapés at parties. He said they were prepared in some God-awful town in the middle of nowhere by really bored and stupid teenagers who couldn't give a stuff about their job, let alone hygiene and health. They were prone to playing the odd practical joke on the unsuspecting scoffer by using impromptu bodily ingredients not generally meant for consumption.

Just on the very edge of the shot, Vance and Edon were having an animated discussion. Then, Thanisi pushed Monaco in the chest and stormed off. Vance headed into the party crowd shaking his head.

"It's so great that we can finally announce our relationship." She gushed when given the cue.

"Good turnout," the crew member said.

"I know. There's Haran, Obi and Morocco for starters."

"Wow, A-listers," said the voice. Not a clue I thought.

"I know right, this is the world I'm now lucky to be in. They're all so lovely but I have to admit to being a bit starstruck."

"Will you get used to it?"

"Oh I think that won't be a problem," she said with complete determination. "This is going to be as popular as the Kardashians."

"What about the age gap?"

"It's just a number. What matters is us spending the rest of our lives together and sharing our lives with all our fans."

"And how's it been going living here together?"

"We love it. I've had a lot to do with the design and there's still a lot more to do."

"Lord Monaco says he's a bit OCD. How do you cope with that?"

"It's quite an adjustment, but we manage it perfectly now. I know what triggers there are and do my best to make sure everything is as it should be. He trusts me implicitly now to do that for him."

Apart from what I'd seen with my own eyes, the programme-makers told me their cameraman heard something interesting. The crew were packing the kit into vans in the drive at 3AM after the party. It had been a long day for them, always worse when all the guests were flying to toy town and they had to work. They had been there 10 hours but finally, the last guests had gone and Vance told them that was their lot, not more filming that morning. The master bedroom window looked out the front of the house. The only lights on were there and Vance and Britney were having a ding-dong. According to the cameraman, he couldn't make out specifics but there was a lot of swearing from them both, screaming from Britney and smashing glass. The crew were too knackered to care and so all got in their van and got out of dodge.

Another bottle had to be opened. It sounds like I'm an alcoholic, but I have had it on medical advice that I'm not. I'm a heavy drinker. The difference? Because I didn't depend on it. However, she said my drinking was just as harmful regarding the liver, cholesterol, blood pressure, etc., basically all the bad stuff. The first time doctor doom asked me about my weekly alcohol unit consumption, she was looking at my blood test results. Knowing that the weekly recommendation was 14, I added a few to make it look natural.

"Eighteen!" I proclaimed.

"Really?" she said much like Ruprecht does in dirty rotten scoundrels.

"Yeah, I know, a little over the top eh doc?" I played the 'Oh you caught me doc' card. She told me that doctors take the units a patient states they consume and then multiply them by 3. I was instructed to dispense with the fantasy world and tell her the truth. When I did, she pretty much gasped.

"It's the Irish in me," I professed. She said there wouldn't be anything in me apart from mush and a vat of alcohol if I went on like that.

The next bit of footage nearly made me drop my glass of vino, nearly. The camera came shakily around a corner to reveal Lady Victoria Monaco in the Kitchen with a drink in her hand. She was laughing and chatting until she saw the camera. Then the scary Medusa came out.

"I told you." She said steely to the poor sap behind the camera, who I imagined had been turned to stone for looking at the Greek Gorgon. The screen went black. What was she doing there? Waking up on the couch at 3am, the wine glass I'd been cradling had been released from my grasp after falling asleep, covering my shirt and cream sofa with its contents. It reminded me that more stain remover from the supermarket was needed.

A Zoom call was the next contact with The Manager. As he appeared on screen, I couldn't help reluctantly admiring the inner confidence of the man, this time wearing a black shirt with bright green apples printed all over it. I'd never been confident in myself, always wanted to be an alpha male with people respecting me. The pilot was all horns / no balls, but here was a true alpha, albeit with psychotic tendencies and Stevie Wonder as his stylist. He didn't give a monkey's what anyone thought about him or his style. But I was going to command this encounter. No jabs to soften him up, straight in with a right hook, I thought.

"Is it true Mr Monaco was looking to move away from your management company?" Nothing, he just stared at me. Talk about starting off well. I was chuffed with the opener, getting one over on this dickhead. "I've discovered he was going to jump ship on you." Again he just stared at the screen. He was playing hardball. Brutal tactics, just silence making the inquisitor doing all the work. I was prepared for that and ready to take this guy on in the stare stakes.

"You're on mute Mr Todd" Bollox! Fuck! I fumbled around, trying to find how the mic had magically turned itself off on my pc. 3 fiddles and three times asking, 'Can you hear me now?' were met with irritated sighs. Finally, I got there and repeated the question.

"Where did you get that?" Bob had been given that little titbit from a member of the drivers' network. This labyrinth of suited vehicle masters was like a secret society. You could spot them outside top restaurants, hotels and some office buildings. They varied in levels depending on who their clients were and what cars they drove. The lower league were the guys who might have been detained At His Majesty's pleasure at some stage in their lives. The top-level operatives, numero unos, were usually ex-forces, trained to kill someone with their little fingers and experts in advanced vehicle evasion techniques. They also had a handgun deposited somewhere about them, even though they weren't allowed to by UK law. Basically, you order an Uber, and The Terminator turns up. Bob was definitely in the former group. However, a level of egalitarian behaviour amongst the brethren existed that was not evident in society in general. When having a smoke while waiting for their charges, every driver would normally talk to another no matter their status. It usually involved comparing their client for the day and moaning about traffic. Another common characteristic was they all knew people. Not like people like Gerry, the accountant who broke out in hives when confronted by anyone. No, they knew people like Dimitri, who would completely ruin your life with a click of a button or Andreas, who'd take you out to the moors, remove your testicles and make you eat them. The people who employed these guys never really gave a fig about them and saw it as just something functional getting to and from places. There were exceptions, of course, drivers who were part of the family, trusted souls and always called by their names. No one really got that nearly all fraternity members were party to information that their clients' closest loved ones wouldn't know. Affairs, deals, threats, violence, money, etc. The code was what one driver told another driver stayed with the recipient – unless that was Bob, thankfully for me.

"I'm afraid it's what I do, Mr Thanisi."

"I'm not a one-trick pony. Vance wasn't my only client. He was a good earner, but I have plenty of good earners."

"Did you do the deal for the TV series?"

"Of course I did. I handle all – handled – all of Vance's business affairs."

"Including selling back catalogues?" I was enjoying this.

"Don't know what you mean. I've got another call I need to take." I saw his finger move to end his side of the convo.

"You didn't tell me you introduced Vance to your sister," I said, throwing a curveball. He suddenly stiffened and withdrew his hand.

"That's personal. Got nothing to do with you."

"Vance left your sister for Ms Chalmers, and that didn't make you mad?"

He moved closer to the camera. "You're overstepping your tiny territory here, Mr Todd." He couldn't conceal the sheer anger bristling in his expression. "Vance was the victim of a terrible accident. Am I sad he's dead? No. Did I kill him? No Colin, I did not. He was not a nice man. He hurt my sister, which is unforgivable where I come from."

"Gloucestershire?" I got him snarling like a cartoon bull with steam coming out his nostrils. "I've seen footage from the doc – you're arguing with Sir Vance. What was that about?"

"Look," he started like politicians do before they talk down to people. He told me that Clause was pissed and upset that Vance was pulling out of the school. He was going to bottle Monaco at the very least and was even eying up the knives in the kitchen. Vance had found out about this and would 'fix it'. All Edon claimed I saw was calming Vance down. He pushed him to make the point that the craziness needed to stop.

"You seemed to be the aggressive one in the footage I saw."

"That's my style, Mr Todd. In my business, if you're not tough, you'll get walked on."

"Did you know about Clause's involvement in the drugs?" his face showed a flicker of emotion – irritation mixed with rage.

"Whatever he does in his free time is not my business. He's a grown man."

"I just think..."

"I don't care what you think but I can tell you – again – I didn't kill him. Simple as that. Now make like a turd and disappear down the toilet back to your sewer."

17

We'd moved to the *Greyhound*, a gastropub a few blocks away from our usual. The *Oak* was closed, not for refurbishment as it should have been, but because pest control was in. A neighbour had seen a rat, apparently the size of a dog, go through the back kitchen door and not come out. We didn't put it past Roger to have caught the rodent and turned it into that week's burgers. We never ate in there and just about trusted the packets of peanuts not to make us do the technicoloured yawn. The pub looked like many other gastro places, all with similar pastel colour schemes and blackboards written in chalk in the same italic style standard with this type of eatery. Bob brought the drinks over.

"Fucking six eighty for a pint?"

"Well that's about right for a place like this," I proffered.

"Is it made from diamonds?" A rhetorical question. He took a sip and shook his head, "Call your mates in the filf and get these lot arrested for robbery."

"So how's the good lady wife?"

"Fucking nightmare."

"Ah."

"She's only asking me what I talk about down the boozer. She's taking an interest she calls it."

"That's good. What's wrong with that?"

"I don't have a scooby (*Scooby Doo – clue*) what we talk about. I'd say football and beer, that's it."

"And the cases, don't forget those."

"I can't tell her I'm working for the filf. She'd rather I shagged someone else than that."

"Well then. Tell her about the beer and football."

"Oh no. Not good enough. One of her mates has become a relationship counsellor," he said, putting the title in fingers inverted commas. "And this bird is filling her with all sorts of shit that don't belong in a marriage. Just leave it will ya for fuck's sake." After he ranted for what seemed like hours and made me wish I'd never asked, he did impart the info he'd garnered. He'd found out about Edon's past. Coming from a very privileged background, he screwed it up. As a youngster, Thanisi had everything he could want without any jeopardy of earning or even losing it. There was a complete absence of life goals or ambitions, not even some nonsense dot com that would burn gazillions and nearly bankrupt the family. He caused a 50-car pileup on the M4 motorway after smashing his Ferrari into the barrier whilst higher than a giraffe's testicles. Papa had a hedge fund friend originally from Albania and still had a large setup there. So that's where young Thanisi (or should I *say Fortesque)* was sent to live. He fell in with the local gangsters. On a trip to Tirana, Edon accidentally killed a prostitute in a sex game. The gang got him out and back to London and made the charges, plus the police, disappear. As such, Edon was in debt to them on returning to the UK. He introduced aviators to them, so he must have known about the drugs then.

"So, aviators and the lady of the manor have been an item for a while now. Seems there all bonking each other." I was sure Britney was blissfully unaware of this but what if aviators found out about it? That would add to his motive – jealousy. We got on to a discussion about how forward-thinking we were when it came to sex. Turns out, I wasn't.

"It's magic when me and the wife are thinking about sex." I didn't really want to hear more.

"Yeah, she disappears." I'm pretty sure it wasn't an original.

On meeting Clause back at the airfield, he insisted we go up in a plane, claiming it was the only way he could think and talk to me. I agreed. Bad mistake. The aircraft was a modern twin-engine propeller with stairs at the front and a ramp door at the back. It was the one in the video on the flying aces website. I half expected to be brushing coke off the seats. We got high up, and I started to feel a little queasy as the vertigo kicked in. Aviators pushed a button that began to lower the ramp at the back. It was like a mini version of the Air Force's big cargo planes.

"Blah blah blah," said Clause. The noise from the wind coming in the now open ramp meant I couldn't make out a word of it.

"Blah blah blah," he said again as he pushed another button and got up from his seat. I'd seen this before on the site, but Clause wasn't wearing a parachute this time, and I was in the plane. The site of him getting up filled me with terror. I grabbed his arm and shouted as loud as I could.

"Sit down!" He stopped, looked at me, smiled, sat back down, and closed the ramp bringing back just a quiet din to the cockpit.

"It's alright man, we're on autopilot," the smug git said, pleased with his stunt. "I was just showing you where Vance jumped from."

"You could have done that from there," I snapped.

"Are you a nervous flyer?"

"When I see the man flying the plane I'm in, get up and leave me up here alone, you could say I'm a fucking nervous flyer, yes." Still in shock, I hadn't immediately noticed that Clause used more than two words.

"This is a great plane you know man. It can cope with anything,"

"What were you arguing with Vance about on the night of the party?"

"What do you mean?"

"Mr Thanisi said you argued with Vance the night before his death."

"So?"

"Which resulted in a scuffle and threats – from you."

"He was going to pull out of the school."

"Couldn't you find other investors, maybe of an Albanian kind?"

"We were making a big loss. No one would take that on."

"Did he find out about your little extra-curriculum activities?"

"My what?"

"Your drug running." I had him. He stared straight ahead in silence, without reaction or moving a muscle. I was going to press him. When you have the upper hand, silence is always a million times better than any other interview technique.

"You know he was going to leave Britney."

"Mr Walner, I'm not here to discuss Ms Chalmers, I want to know about the drugs." His head stayed fixed, looking straight ahead.

"These planes are great you know," he said after an age but without moving a muscle.

"He found out about your deal with the gangsters and that was why he was pulling out of the business. You lose him, you lose the school and the bad guys, which would be the final nail in your coffin of debt."

"Even a freefall," with that, he threw the joystick forward sharply. I was suddenly looking out of the windscreen with the ground filling the whole of it. My insides had been moulded to the back of the seat, and blood rushed to my head making me dizzy as I screamed. Then suddenly, it felt like we were momentarily weightless, floating in the cockpit. Despite my disorientation and sheer terror, I did wonder if the pilot had a suicidal streak and we were never really going to talk. We were going to hurtle to the ground much like Vance did but this time still in the aeroplane. With a pullback on the joystick, the whole windscreen was this time, filled with the grey sky as we pointed directly upwards.

What was this guy doing to me? Then just like that, we were level again. I was shaking. My fingers had penetrated the seat's leather as I gripped it in sheer terror.

"I'll tell you something about Vance Monaco." Clause was just staring straight ahead.

"What was that you arsehole?"

"Vance was a psycho."

"He's not the only one. Take us down." Clause didn't move and I had no way of getting him to do it, not unless I was going to wrestle control off him which would most certainly kill us both.

"I was totally bombed at the party man," he said, removing his sunglasses.

"But you were going to attack him because he was closing the flying school."

"I wasn't going to attack him."

"Edon said he stopped you smashing a bottle over his head."

"Did he also tell you that those two weren't exactly best of buds."

"In what way?"

"The snake (that's Thanisi)..."

"I gathered that."

"Was losing the main source of his folding. He was setting up his own management company."

"I'm aware of the situation."

"But that meant any new accountant looking at the books would have seen various amounts coming out of Monaco's accounts."

"Where did these amounts end up?"

"Various offshore accounts controlled by Thanisi."

"That doesn't take away from the fact that with the school closing, you were in trouble with the gang, the sort of trouble that doesn't go away – so you had to make Mr Monaco go away. You cut his risers on the evening of the party. Problem solved"

"Once you're in, you're in. The only way out is cement boots."

18

An email from the client:

Mr Todd, expect a package to be delivered. In it are instructions and keys.

Then I got a text message from DHL with tracking for a parcel that was being delivered the next day. They helpfully stated it would be delivered between 0800 – 1800, so the whole day then. I'd spent so much time tracking delivery drivers as they neared my address, and although the map showed they were only around the corner, they still had 50 more stops to go. Then if I didn't open the door as soon as they rang the buzzer, they'd bugger off. It so happened with this package. I was on the loo when the buzzer went. Being halfway through, there was no way I could have done the necessary in time to answer them. A rearranged delivery came the next day, and I was waiting like a coiled spring by the front door. As soon as he pulled up, I was on him like a Barcelona pickpocket. The package looked a bit like those parcels angry people used to send Anthrax to various people around the world. It would have caused a few alarms to go off in airport security. Inside was a single piece of A4 with printed words and a set of keys. The printed paper had the address of someplace in Kitzbuhel in Austria and how to get in using the provided keys. I was to go and inspect the place Lord and Lady M owned together for 20 years and still did. I questioned the need to go at all but my benefactor insisted. As the manager said, 'How high?'

Due to my financial situation, I went for a budget airline (the lowest one) from Luton and solemnly vowed never to do it again. 'London' Luton airport is basically a couple of shipping containers bolted together, nowhere near London and filled with the people you only see in service stations. Feral children, obnoxious parents, mess, noise and everyone dressed in knock-off trackies. Most of the adults (and some of the young kids) on the flight were completely ratarsed. So fights broke out between the males and screaming matches between overweight women wearing 'relaxing' leggings because they couldn't find anything else to get over their enormous lower halves. 'It's not fucking worth it Chardonnay' was heard a few times. Whilst carnage was breaking out with the parents, the offspring were throwing up because they'd slammed down a couple of snakebite and blacks at the airport. One such waste of air was sitting beside me. As the stench wafted up from his vomit, this forced me to be sick too. The smell will always make me react so. I was a sympathetic puker. The sight, and particularly the smell, made me heave in solidarity. So the young chav with that just-out-of-prison look and I were utilising our sick bags together. Every time he expelled and the smell came up, so did I.

"Please God, stop it you little fucker!" I shouted. This angered his mum in front, who tried to grab me over the seat, but the amount of flesh hanging off her bones prevented ascendency. The dad was too busy telling his mates some story about how Dylan had been stabbed. Although I had coshed myself well before the flight with a rather strong Valium, that still didn't negate the horror of the zoo at 35,000 feet. From that flight onwards, unless I was going business class, I would rather not go. I didn't care if it meant never going abroad again because it just wasn't worth it.

Kitzbuhel was a very upmarket ski resort famed for royals of all countries, the rich and, of course, Vance. What I took away from my first-ever visit there was that the Austrians were batshit crazy – in the good way. Despite their love of the most annoying boom boom music, something used as a torture method in Guantanamo, they had a disregard for rules that would make a Frenchman blush. They smoked heavily (at the bar - sheer heaven), and when confronted with the choice of not having schnapps or chopping their hands off, they'd go for the missing limb option. Beer was drunk at 9am, with smokes of course. Cardiologists were in scant demand as potential heart attack victims just didn't care. The goulash and schnitzel were genuinely superb. There were no vegans in Austria. The taxi driver from the airport pretended to speak no English even though most Germans and Austrians put everyone else to shame by speaking several languages, English as a second language. That didn't matter because I wasn't in a convo mood. I was screaming 'Fuuuuckkkk'. He'd decided not to bother with normal road rules and went into that taxi driver I will shit this guy up mode. As he took blind bends on the wrong side of windy roads, he stared at me in the rearview mirror, meaning of course, he wasn't looking to see if the next bend was on course to turn us into schnitzel. I hoped an equally unhinged cabbie was coming the other way so they'd both miss each other because they were equally on the wrong side. We stopped at a petrol station, and they had a beer at the counter, something new on me at a roadside garage. I grabbed a six-pack to allow me to continue the journey without needing the brown trousers.

It was midsummer, so there was no snow in the very pretty town or the mountains that towered above it. The place was set at the foot of a valley, surrounded by (now green) alpine splendour. It was the picture postcard old village you'd expect in the Alps, all wood, old buildings, cobbled streets and not a sign of a Pret in sight. Because it wasn't the high ski season, gone were the horse-drawn carriages that ferried tourists around for the price of an average house. Gone too, were the people. As a ski resort, that was their reason for existence. The summer lot all wanted to hike and mountain bike (and the lifts opened for that) but they were 1/10 of the number of visitors. When Kitzbuhel hosted the world cup downhill skiing event (the infamous Hahnenkamm), people would have to stay in towns 40 miles away as there was no room at the inn. By the time I arrived after the flight from hell, it was too late to go searching the chalet so what else was there to do but go to the pub. This one was bang in the middle of the main square. A circular bar surrounded by chairs and tables six deep. Around the circumference of the drink dispensing bit were tall stools. I got talking to a guy, Alan, who was the archetypal hobby cyclist. He had all the gear, no idea. Fully kitted out with all the lycra, gloves, etc., even though it was dark. His Batman-looking bike was locked up on the other side of the street. He'd been cycling all day, and his 'thighs hurt like fuck. But worth it right.' I guessed his wife didn't share his passion for two wheels.

"She's in Ibiza, lying on a beach doing fuck all and drinking cocktails," he sniffed.

"Sounds way better to me."

"Torture. What a waste of life." They, and we, were clearly not on the same page re leisure time, and I immediately knew who would have been having a better time. It wasn't Alan. He went to the toilet, walking awkwardly because of those cycling shoes that lock into the pedals. They made all the difference when a hobbyist cyclist got his fat arse into lycra and on a bike. As he clacked off, the barman laughed and shook his head in disgust. By the time Lance Armstrong returned, I had discovered that the barman was called Woody. A plan hatched in my stupid mind. When Alan perched his lycra on the stool again, that was my moment.

"Woody," I said, looking at the barman and gesturing to him. He looked up from doing a drink. "Alan," I said, gesturing to the cycling man. They both looked at each other.

"Hi," said Alan. Woody looked at me as though he'd just found out he was a father. He looked back at Alan, who was nonplussed by the silence. Then the barkeep burst out laughing. Not a timid little laugh, one that made him double over in uncontrollable hysterics, banging the counter that was now minus the drink he'd been preparing because he'd knocked it over. I joined in. Alan didn't and was still unsure about the joke, even after repeated explanations. Woody even got the owners out of the restaurant inside to repeat the feat. I was rather proud of myself. We drank free schnapps and Jagermeister in many forms until 2am. When Alan got on his bike and crashed it straight into a wall, no one rushed to his aid. We were too busy laughing.

The following day was not good. Having mixed all sorts of stuff I never usually drank, I had one of those new hangovers, the ones where the body says, 'You what? I'm not used to that shit. I will fuck you up all day for this.' The first thing that struck me, I was on my back on the top of the single bed, still in my clothes. It was supposed to be a double, but an Austrian double means a gymnastic beam. I had no sensation of feeling in my mouth. This wasn't caused by the flaming thing we had a few rounds of but the fact that it had been wholly starved of moisture and oxygen as I snored like a pig in my deep, alcohol-induced slumber. I tried to grab the water on the side table but fell off the bed, so decided to go back to sleep there and then.

It took until lunchtime until I could surface from the hostel-like cheap accommodation. There were jolly people in the bar opposite having a beer, as they always were in Austria. There was only one way out of my hangover hell, and it was presented to me in the form of a bar. An hour later, I made my way to the chalet. Prime real estate in this town was very, very expensive. The best ones were not in the centre but in what could be described as the suburbs, even though they were a 10-minute walk from the square. They were big and stacked up the hill. The main reason for these places being the desired location was that in the snow, people staying there could ski down to the central lifts from their back door and then, at the end of the day, ski straight back to the chalet. Chalet, boots on, ski, nice lunch, chalet, boots off, champagne and hot tub. Terrible right.

It had everything you'd expect of an Alpine retreat, mainly consisting of a lot of wood, thick white rugs and a massive fireplace. The furniture had clearly been given a reboot. It was modern and expensive. I still had no idea what I was supposed to be looking for, so wandered about aimlessly, opening drawers. Three hours later, with nothing of note to show for it, I decided it was time to give up. The client really should have directed me to the pot of gold at the end of the rainbow if she wanted me to find it. Time for a quick visit to the loo before leaving. I entered what was a shrine to the Monacos in pictures. Every inch was covered in pictures, a record of the A-listers throughout the decades that had been in their lives. Him meeting a couple of US Presidents, getting his knighthood from the Queen, and shaking hands with the Pope in the Vatican, for example. One I particularly liked was a framed Irish Times front page. It was from when Thunderbolt visited Dublin in the 80s, provoking mass hysteria amongst vast swathes of Irish teenage girls. Central to the piece was a black & white picture of a shirtless Monaco in a nightclub with two scantily clad women on his knee. They were wearing 'Miss Kerry' and 'Miss Dublin' The trio were pouring magnums of Dom Perignon over each other's heads whilst holding cigarettes. It was one of the most iconic images of the decade. Women wanted to be with him, and men wanted to be him. The text underneath the picture just said, 'Where did all go so wrong Vance?'. Then there was one that stunned me. It was Vance outside a plane in parachute gear. With him were the Pilot and a Hollywood actor even I recognized, which meant he was very famous indeed. Big deal, I hear you say, Vance, going skyfalling. The interesting part was the fourth member of the party. Also in a jumpsuit, holding a helmet, in a harness, and laughing heartily - it was the wife. Underneath the photo, the caption said, 'Monaco and his wife were joined at the regular parachute jump by Hollywood star Harrison White.' This must have been what the client wanted me to see. So she'd lied to me about skydiving. Along with the motive of losing Vance's cash and the access, she now had the knowledge to do the crime. Keen to get my middle-class inferiority complex knocked on the head, I would question her again about this humdinger of information

19

The reopened Oak & Saw looked precisely the same. However, it did have a different musky smell on account of the rat poison sprayed into the cavities between the walls. John assured us all was safe, but we couldn't help but notice he had a World War two gas mask under the bar. I threw my current thoughts out to Bob.

"Perhaps The Manager and the pilot were in this together? They both had the connection - and debt with the gangsters. All of them had a vested interest in seeing the back of Sir Vance. So Edon and Clause said they'd sort it and conspired to kill him with a murder that no one would ever find evidence of. Thanisi gets control of the business interests, aviators doesn't go to jail and the Albanians get off both their backs."

"Still flyboy for me."

"What about the Lady of the manor?" Her family were cash poor, so for Lady Victoria to lose the inheritance from Monaco would be a massive blow to her and the daughter who lived in Florida.

"Nah, she ain't the type."

"Oh, I think she could be."

"Ice running through them veins of hers, but the toffs stick with their husbands. She's still in deep with him, in more ways than one eh."

"Where did you get your psychology degree? Walmart?"

"Alight, you're Colombian. Who do you fink did it?"

"Columbian?"

"Yeah, you know the detective with the mac and cigar, oh one more question."

"Columbo."

"What I said."

"Well, I'm meeting Lady Monaco again tomorrow."

"Take bollox protection."

"Oh I've got her for lying to me."

"This case reminds me of my cousin, Geoff."

I regrettably asked, "How come?"

"Well, he was proper straight geezer, never in trouble or nothing." I doubted that. "Then he gets framed for murdering his wife. Escapes from a prison transport, looking to prove his innocence while this cop hunts him down." I just nodded. Apart from having no correlation at all, of course, that was Harrison Ford's excellent movie, the fugitive.

"A quick question."

"What?"

"Do you watch anything other than action movies?"

"My wife keeps having a go at me for my bad Arnie film references, but don't worry, I'll return."

The venue for my second meeting with Lady Monaco was the Ritz for afternoon tea – her choice. I always thought this was something tourists did in London, thinking it was what the Queen had every day. No person would make it past 40 if they did that. The associated calorie intake would see to a guaranteed heart attack. Walking up to reception, I received the customary snooty look. However, as soon as Victoria's name was mentioned, it was suddenly all smiles and deference. I was shown to where the grand dame was waiting. On the table was what could only be described as a mountain loveliness – sandwiches, 10 different types, all cut into beautifully precise triangles minus their crusts.

They fanned out over plates on a stand that rose into the sky in a Christmas tree shape. The same arrangement was given to the best-looking scones, accompanied by pots of cream, jam, and tea accoutrements. A glass of champagne sat nearest to m 'lady's teacup. She stayed seated and extended her hand (palm down) for me to shake. We exchanged pleasantries and general small talk.

"Would you like more tea, Mr Todd?"

"I'm good thanks."

"I'll be the judge of that." She saw my confusion at what was meant. "I'll be the judge of whether you're good or not. You don't make that call." The very definition of an aunt from PG Woodhouse or even Hera from Greek mythology sat before me.

"Can I ask?"

"You can try."

"Why were you at the party the night before Vance's death?"

"What?" Ahah, I had something to spring on her.

"Well, I saw you in the rushes of the TV documentary that night at the party. You told the cameraman to stop filming, which he did as though his life depended on it." She fixed me a silent gaze as she deliberated how to answer.

"I'm a very private person. My family and I don't like publicity."

"But why were you there?" She summoned a waiter by raising a finger, not averting her gaze from me. They were already carrying a bottle of champagne and filled her glass without any instructions or words exchanged.

"My catering business, we were doing the party so as the MD, I needed to be there to ensure all went well."

"That's very nice of Sir Vance, seeing you got the business."

"He was a very kind man." I dolloped a load of the cream on a perfectly halved scone.

"Oh, you're a Devonshire man."

"No, I'm from Ireland."

"It's just Devonshire folk opt for cream then jam but Cornwall folk – and Her Majesty, do jam then cream." I started to feel a hint of genuine dislike to this patronizing harpy.

"What about Mr Walner? Where does he fit in?" She looked at me, almost recognizing my efforts.

"At first it was revenge for one of the many affairs Vance had – have one with the guy he looks up to"

"He looked up to Clause?"

"For some godforsaken reason. Vannie often wished he'd never been well-known at all. He would have given his right arm to have a pint in that horrid place of yours."

"He might never have got it back."

"He didn't like being famous, but without it, there'd be no money, no house in the south of France, no ski chalet..."

"...or groupies down on their knees," Shit! It just came out. It was my third glass of champagne, so my self-editing facility had somewhat diminished. I immediately regretted it, but such an utterance didn't faze her at all.

"Indeed Mr Todd." I tried to rescue myself.

"I believe he was changing his will to leave most of his estate to a conspiracy theory group called, er called..."

"CRAP" This woman made me nervous.

"That's them."

She got up to leave, surrounded by waiting staff to usher her off to the cloakroom. "Your problem is that you can make up whatever theory you like as to who murdered Vance if anyone did, but you then have to prove it, don't you?"

"Quick question."

"Yes," she spat, stopping in her tracks at the edge of the table. Time for the knockout blow.

"You said you didn't skydive, but I've seen the picture from the 80s with you, him, Edon, and Clause. You're all in parachute gear with parachutes on your back. Looked to me as if you might possibly be going parachuting?" A deep sigh from her as she adjusted her blouse, then shot me a death stare.

"I told you I don't jump out of perfectly working aeroplanes. Present tense Mr Todd. I did a few back in the day, possibly 15 years ago."

Mulling the case back at the flat from another unsuccessful date. That one had ended when she said that the Vagina candle from perpetual looney Gwyneth Paltrow was a priceless gift to womankind. There was still an irritation hanging around. It nagged me like waking up in the dark to hear a mosquito making passes at my head. The big e – evidence – or to be more precise, a complete lack of it. Motives, access, and expertise were all there for the main suspects, but I was worried about pulling them all together.

Pub time.

"You ain't got a Danny, have ya? *(Danny - Danny La Rue- Clue).* It could be any of 'em right?"

"Thanks for the valuable input Bob. I'll park it in a safe space to revisit at a later stage."

"Well, Alfred Einstein, who did do it then?"

"OK, I don't fucking know!"

"Language, there are kiddies about." Of course there weren't. The truth was that I would have to hand the money back to the client. This prospect was a big problem, I'd already spent most of the fee. All the suspects had access, the proper knowledge, and motive. I just couldn't find any evidence at all that linked one of them to the demise of the music Knight of the Realm.

This, in essence, was why the police decided to not bother with a lengthy investigation. The British legal system requires the prosecution in any criminal case to prove, beyond all reasonable doubt, that the accused was guilty. Any doubt in the mind of the jury means the prosecution didn't do that and so the person on trial is thus a free person. Sometimes a Judge can accept a majority verdict, but that's not the norm or what is enshrined in our case law legal system. I'd been in many courts where the quality of the barrister or barristers, either defending or prosecuting, had a direct and quantifiable effect on the minds and thus the verdict of the jury. Those guys and girls, looking a tad ridiculous in wigs and gowns, were highly skilled in what they did. Not just any muppet could do the job. Everything they did and said in court was for effect, to help their client and influence the judge and jury in their favour. Like every job in life though, there were the terrible ones who usually got their clients sent to prison up to the really amazing ones who named newly-built wings on their country estates after the clients they'd just been paid a king's ransom to defend – it was usually defending rather than prosecute. In this case, even a bad one could hit a home run. All they needed to say was, 'Members of the jury, it really could have been any one of them. Where is the evidence linking my client to that actual act of cutting the risers? If you have any doubt as to whether there is enough, if not any, evidence linking my client to this act, as I'm sure you will have, then you have no other option but to acquit my client.' Case over.

Bob got philosophical. "Aint life a shitter." I had to agree. "I got sommink to cheer you up.," He unlocked his gigantic phone that had a screen bigger than my laptop. "Take a butcher's (*Butcher's Hook- Look)* at this," he said as a black and white video appeared. It was one of the pub CCTV cameras showing the bar square on. Standing with their backs to the camera were Happy Larry (the man who constantly moaned about everything) and his wife, Tyson, who was known to be handy with her fists. A blonde girl wearing very short shorts, a tight t-shirt, and a rucksack entered the shot. She approached the bar, stood beside Happy, and started talking to John. Bob explained, "Banging hot tourist asking for directions,". Like Benny Hill, Larry starts staring at her pert behind, bending back and sideways to get the best view. The poor girl was oblivious to the attention, but Tyson wasn't. She clocks her other half letching and slaps him so hard in the face that Larry falls to the floor behind the tourist. Bullshit started laughing hysterically. "Proper did him". The young girl appears to scream and runs out in horror. Tyson just picked her drink up and took a sip. "How funny is that! I'm so going to give it loads to him later."

"Later? How long ago was this taken?"

"Last week," he says as he starts the video again chuckling violently.

"But I thought John had disconnected the CCTV cameras?" I asked.

"He only disconnected the network because it was stopping his son having a tommy *(tommy tank - wank)* to porn." His son was 40 and still lived upstairs with John.

"But how can they still record?"

"Ah for fuck's sake!" He stopped the video with a sigh and put his phone down.

"The cameras are connected to a server via the Wi-Fi." When it came to technology, my Grandad was better. "The server takes all their feeds, sorts 'em, and records 'em."

"But if they're disconnected from that server, how do you still get that video?"

"They have internal memory cards and because they're motion-sensitive, they can record months of stuff on 'em." Then, as I sprinted out the door like Usain Bolt, I heard Bob shouting, "Where the fu...."

20

I still had the alarm instructions for Monaco's Warwickshire pad. I needed to get down there. Bob's little video had given me hope. Perhaps, just perhaps, although all his cameras were disconnected from the server, their internal memory cards could still have been recording. They could hold vital evidence that would help me finally crack the case. The ticket machines at Paddington were playing up, creating a bottleneck around the only working one. I was impatient, jumping up and down like a child needing the toilet. Why was it always the case at times like these, the human race's stupidest people got in your way. The five people in front of me did their best impressions of a row of single-cell amoebas. They possessed an innate inability to deal with the touchscreen, navigate the menu, find, select and pay for their tickets. That definitely wasn't good for my high blood pressure.

Finally, I arrived at the gates, armed again with the alarm instructions on my phone. The housekeeper was suspicious as to why I needed to go back there. It had taken frustrating calls with her on the train. I hit what must have been the stretch of railway line with the largest number of bridges in the UK. We kept getting cut off, but eventually, she relented and said it would be OK. There wouldn't be anyone there, which suited me. Once in, the first thing to strike me was how cold it was. Not so much temperature; it was 70 degrees outside, but in atmosphere. A house gets like that when there hasn't been human activity in it for a while. All furniture, personal items and anything related to Monaco had been removed. The soul of the place had been put in a deep freeze.

Standing in the vast, cavernous hallway, something worrying struck me as I stared up at a couple of cameras. Well, two things actually. First, I had no idea how to extract the memory cards from the cameras, and second, how would I even get up to them. The first dilemma required Bob's input.

"Have a look for something that looks as though it slides out of the casing," he advised.

"How am I supposed to see that?"

"Just use your thumb and explore. Try sliding bits to see if they give."

"It's twelve feet in the air."

"Wot, you ain't holding one right now?"

"I've got to find a way to get up to them first."

"For fuck's sake Porot," he shouted and hung up.

A search through all the hallway doors revealed nothing I could use to ascend to the prizes and their much-needed bounty. A set of French doors led out to the vast patio, bridging the space between the lush garden and the house. Standing in the middle of the stone expanse, a beautiful garden filled the horizon beyond. I spied a shed the size of a small house and thought it might be worth a try. Brilliant luck. Whoever cleared the house had left a solitary ladder in there with only itself for company. On exiting the shed door, something stood in my way between me and the house. It was a snarling, muscly Alsatian. A slight presence of foam around its mouth gave off the air of being a tad rabid. We stood, staring at each other. It wouldn't be a tough guess whether man or beast was the scared one. With one hand, I moved the ladder in front of me to act as some sort of shield should the canine attack. With the other, I slowly reached behind me to grab the shed door handle. Then it lept forward. I threw the ladder at it and managed to get back into the shed. A thud indicated it had run into the closed wooden obstacle. Rabies must have messed with its noggin.

"Wot you want me to do about it? I'm in London dick'ed." Bob wasn't very helpful. The housekeeper informed me it was the neighbour's dog that kept getting out. It wasn't rabid, just unfriendly. That didn't help my situ though. I could hear him snarling and pacing about outside. Finally, after an hour, it seemed Fido had given up and gone elsewhere. Peeping through a slightly ajar door, I could see no sign of my nemesis, so decided to run for the house, picking up the ladder on the way. Halfway home, the hound appeared from the bushes, barking and running at full pelt. I quickly surmised it would get to me before I could get to safety, so I readied myself with the ladder as a weapon. With a lunge, it went for my leg. With a swipe, I connected squarely with its head. Without even a whimper, it fell to the ground. I rushed into the house and could see from the French Doors there was no movement from it. I'd worry about that later. I needed those cameras.

Health and safety videos and briefings always talk about anchoring a ladder (by someone or an object) to aid the climber in doing whatever he needed to do up there. There's an excellent reason for that advice. Having not seen the direction beforehand, I set the ladder against the wall underneath the first camera. Its feet were on the marble floor. When I got level with the camera, I reached for it with a move that exerted pressure through my feet on the rung I was standing on. Newton's Third Law dictates that for every action (force), there is an equal and opposite reaction. My school physics teacher would have been proud that theory was proved when the ladder disappeared from underneath me. To save myself from ending up in A&E, I grabbed at the camera to provide a modicum of purchase. It worked – for about a second. Then, it gave way, depositing me and it on the marble floor. After ascertaining I hadn't hurt anything, I looked at the camera smashed to smithereens around me. A tiny bit of plastic in the wreckage looked like a memory card. I knew it was because it had '4k Memory Card' printed on it. The ladder would perform like that every time on these floors, so I found another use for it that killed two birds with one stone. I'd use it to smash the cameras off their perches by whacking them with it and coughing u cards in the smashed bits. A dog and the cameras, this ladder had multi-uses. I figured my client wouldn't mind if I created a bit of a mess, as long as it was sorted out afterwards, if it solved the case.

At the end of the day, after therapeutic smashing carnage had been carried out, the dog had gone. I had one more camera to go, the one in the parachute room. There were no parachutes in there. It was a sad sight. Skydiving, by its very nature, was full of thrills and adrenaline. When I saw the inanimate backpacks in the documentary lined up in that room, they still represented what their use would be: going nuts and being free. Not now. This camera was the one, the one giving me the smoking gun, the person who cut the risers. It could only have happened here, in this room, and that camera must have recorded it. I left the house via the front door to get in the waiting Uber that would ferry me to the station. I'd forgotten about the Alsatian. It hadn't forgotten about me. It appeared from nowhere, snarling for all its worth. I ran for the car and just got in in time. I was up face to face with the enormous gnashers as the canine tried to get at me through the window.

"Drive!" The terrified driver stepped on it. It gave up chasing us after a mile.

Back at my flat, the cat came through the cat flap as I was looking at all twenty of the memory cards on my kitchen table. A favourite claret had been cracked open in celebration.

"This is it Bubbles. These cameras have recorded the whole night. Who did it eh?" I felt something on my foot and looked down to where a wriggling mouse had been dropped. My instinctive reaction was to yelp and kick out, causing the rodent to go airborne and hit the wall hard. It fell to the floor motionless. Bubbles sauntered over to it, sniffed, poked with a paw, saw no movement, and then headed off to the litter tray. If you're wondering why a cat with access to the outside still uses a litter tray, that's another story. Having put the poor little critter in the garden, hoping it was just stunned, my attention turned to memory cards again. Oh, what these guys could tell me.

When I took them to Bob in the pub (what a shock eh) I was more hopeful than a guy called Hope, who lived in Hopeville on the planet of Hope. He attached a card-reading device to a laptop, and away we went.

"Which cards are the parachute room then?"

"I don't know."

"You didn't number 'em as you got 'em or at least make a note?"

I could see that would have been the smart thing to do. "Fuck's sake. Ok, lucky dip. Let's start with this one," he said, picking a card and put it into the reader. Nothing happened on the laptop screen.

"Is your computer broken?" I asked.

"All right Will Gates, you wanna do it?"

"Sorry, carry on."

"Thanks your highness. We have to go through them all to find the ones that were still recording." He did some tapping, removed the card from the reader, picked another one off the table, and inserted it.

Whilst we waited for something to happen on the laptop, I asked Bob a question. "You don't think I look like Harry, do you?"

"Twins. Well, his older twin." I wished Bob had lived up to his name and spun me some pony *(pony and trap - crap)* about not resembling him so closely. I vowed to get rid of the beard. Suddenly an image popped up on the laptop with one of the cards.

"Here we go sunshine, we're in." The black and white picture of a door popped up. "A door, brilliant."

"No, that door is the one leading to the parachute room. Only one way in, so we'll get the killer entering."

"Cushtie."

This first image was from three months before Vance's skyfalling for the last time. "Bollox!" Bob said. The picture went black. "Camera's gone off. Battery must have died." We went through the rest of the cards. Many had similar problems, hadn't recorded anything, or were useless angles. We got down to two left. The penultimate one worked but was of the garage. Apart from drivers and Vance getting in and out of cars, nothing of note was on them. One left. Please, please be the parachute room.

"Does the prof get the murderer or a shit sandwich?" Bob said as he stuck the card in. What seemed like an eternity elapsed until the laptop showed an image. Yes, it was the one I wanted. The angle was quite tight (I'd picked up some TV terms), meaning that the camera didn't take in the whole room. It was focused on the centre of the line of parachutes but the ones on the edges were only partially in shot. I had no idea which parachute in that line was the fatal one, but if it was any of the ones on the end of the line, we wouldn't get a good image of them being cut.

"Where shall we start?"

"Go to a couple of days before the jump." He spooled it to two days before. Then we watched it at double the speed. Nothing happened much. Cleaners were wandering in and out, Vance wandering in out, Britney wandering in and out. All normal, then we got to the morning of the party and put the playback at one and a half the speed. At 10:54:34, we saw Vance tidying the parachute packs. They already looked in precise formation, but he went down the line in the ones we could see, just using his hands to make sure all were exactly level. He pulled out the one in the centre, opened the flap, checked it, ten times, and then left it out in front of the other rucksacks in the row. Then he left, turning the light off. Nothing further came up until the appearance I'd been waiting for finally came. At 01:10:12, a figure appeared as the lights went on. The figure was wearing a black hoodie, hood up, and the hands were covered with surgical gloves.

The person stopped in the centre of the line and picked up the one in the middle. They expertly undid the shoulder straps exposing the risers. Suddenly there was a flash of a blade in the right hand and the unmistakable hand motion of sawing in the area of the risers on the right-hand side. Then they moved to the left-hand side with the same action. That was it! We had the actual act of murder happening before our very eyes.

"Yes! We've got them Bob. Bang to rights." I backslapped heartily.

"You got shit man."

"No, we got the person who murdered Vance right there on camera cutting the risers."

"Oh yeah, who is it then?" Bob was right, and it was like a massive kick in the region down below, winding me as though someone had done that wearing metal boots. We could only see the arms and the back of the hoodie covering the head. The murderer hadn't given us the benefit of showing their face, and the camera angle meant we never would see it.

Bob gave me the card reader, and I spent all night going through every ounce of available footage. Tired, pissed, and utterly deflated, I thought it was there at one stage when a long black sleeve top was spotted on the manager. It turned out to be a false lead. I awoke, as usual, on the couch with the traditional deposited glass of red down my front. The video of the murderous act was still playing on a loop, just repeating itself over and over again, reminding me of how close but how far I'd fallen short. Having run out of cigarettes, I picked a half-smoked one from the overflowing ashtray and stared at the screen whilst exhaling. As the smoke cleared, something miraculous happened – literally seeing the wood from the trees. The flash of the blade had taken all my attention. I'd become obsessed with it, but that diverted my focus from the real identifying image. The slam-dunk. At the base of the knife handle, clearly visible in the footage, there was a Japanese inscription in white letters. I'd seen it before. It was on the knife Britney won as a prize for filleting a fish in the jungle show.

21

Before we get on to Britney, what about the others? The Pilot was trapped - torn by the money he made on the drug runs and fear of a horrible death, so he kept doing those flights. When he did that crazy freefall in the plane, he was doing more than just being an arse. He was thinking about ending it all for real. I would have just been a bonus casualty in his death wish. He loved Lady Monaco. I felt sorry for him on that one. It was her who told him that Vance was leaving Britney. But the thought of his love pulled him, and not forgetting me, out of the need to examine the ground at speed in a perpendicular fashion. Monaco didn't find out about the drugs until a few days before his death, when he was already in an advanced state of paranoia. Being let down by a guy he actually looked up to sent the singer into a rage. That's what Monaco and Walner were arguing about at the party, and Vance was the aggressor. It was also the reason why he was taken off the fateful flight. I felt sorry for Clause. The gambling, hopeless love for a woman who didn't love him at all, and being on a never-ending merry-go-round that he just wanted to get off. I didn't include the incriminating drug stuff in my report; it'd be impossible to prove anyway. He disappeared (not in the bad way), and reports were he ran a helicopter ski operation in the Alps.

Thanisi had been my number one suspect. There were so many aspects to his motive, the most incriminating being the fact that he had been embezzling Monaco's money, not just stealing it for himself but washing it for the gangsters he'd introduced the pilot to. With everything stacking up, Edon was sickeningly right about something; he didn't kill his client. He was not a nice man at all and needed to be brought to book. Based on my report, the Met arrested him for theft and money laundering. He got 15 years in prison.

At one stage, I did think the wife might have done it, but she simply wasn't the sort of person who could commit murder. Vance had expressed an intention to leave his estate to CRAP, thus leaving her and the daughter without a penny which supported an excellent motive. He had, in fact, moved it around as a tax-efficient way of being able to leave as much as possible to Lady Monaco and the kid. She still had an unbreakable bond with her rockstar, even if he was off sewing his oats off somewhere else. CRAP carried on the fight of JAQing minus Vance's money.

So on to Britney. She was going to be the new Kim Kardashian, or so she thought. But hearing from Clause that Vance was going to dump her put a massive spanner in those works. The Pilot spilt the beans because he was worried about Lady Monaco getting back with her ex, thus him losing the woman he loved. Somehow, he hoped blabbing would result in that not happening. Britney was faced with all her dreams and ambitions being crushed if they were not an item; the TV show depended on it. As just another younger ex of the legendary lothario, no one would be bothered. D or even F list stardom beckoned where she'd be lucky to get a booking on a celeb antique TV show where everyone watching would ask, 'Who's that?'

Driven by a wave of inner anger about the impending dumping, and a deep sense of revenge for the end of her dreams as a superstar, the plan was hatched. With her experience of parachuting in the jungle show, she knew about risers, their positioning, and how to sort them. Being tee-total, she was in the perfect position to slip down to the parachute room when Vance and the guests were comatose. The black hoodie wasn't anything clever to avoid detection; it was actually her pyjama top. The gloves, however, were. The need for them had been gleaned from online research. Job done, she replaced the backpack in precisely the same place - to the millimetre – and returned to bed.

Using that knife she won from the jungle show to slice the risers was a sense of satisfaction for her. The blade symbolised the start of her journey to fame and fortune. If she hadn't been on the Jungle Love show, she wouldn't have been at the party where she first met Monaco. But she wasn't going to be with him anymore, so what better to take revenge than to kill him using the knife from the show. When I bumped into her at Monaco's house, she wasn't removing sex toys. She was getting rid of the murder weapon. It was later recovered by the police in the lake situated halfway down the mansion drive.

Why didn't she know about the camera? Like us all, she thought with Vance taking the cameras off the network, it wouldn't be working. Having dealt with Vance's OCD and managing it successfully, he trusted her when she told him the chute had been checked, and so when Edon asked about it at the airfield, he was sure the required had been done.

On the morning of the jump, with Vance still unaware Britney knew of his intentions about the relationship, she sent him off with a kiss, knowing he was going to his death. She never got hurt. She got even!

Lady Monaco wanted to meet. Out of respect, I should have gone to meet her at one of the swanky clubs, but childishly, I wanted to make her slum it with a second visit to the open sore. Bob was with me pre-arrival of her majesty.

"Anyway, we make quite a team Porot," he chose to ignore my earlier corrections. I chose to ignore it too.

"Thanks for your help, Bob."

"You can't do this shit without me."

"Well, I don't think…"

Then she walked in, and her presence was felt straight away. If Moses had asked her advice about how to part the Red Sea, she would tell him to stand there, and it would just happen. Walking behind her was another well-dressed woman.

"Lady Monaco, so good to see you."

"Mr Todd," she said as we shook hands. "And?" she asked, looking at Bob.

"Oh, this is Bob. He helped out on this case." He offered his hand up. She was at least 5 inches taller than him, as was anyone over the age of 10 years old. He was almost reverent; in a way a serf would have been meeting the lord of the manor back in ancient times.

"And this is Jenny Savage. You spoke with her on the phone,"

"Ah yes, Ms Savage, good to meet you."

"Oh please, it's Jenny," I had purposely left two of the worst stools in the pub on the other side of the table (I woke up the next day thinking what a dick I was being so petty). Jenny sat down straight away. Like Bubbles, Lady Monaco circled the stool and eventually sat down like she was hovering over a spike.

"I would like to say we're very pleased you managed to get to the bottom of this."

"All in a day's work Lady Monaco," Bob snorted disdain. "And what do I owe the pleasure of this visit?

"I thought you may be curious as to who your client was." Now my time to get the upper hand on her.

"Oh, I know who it is."

"Oh really! Pray tell who?" Time for my coup de grace.

"You." There was no reaction from the ice maiden, but Jenny laughed loudly and then cupped her mouth. She couldn't stop laughing and Bob joined in.

"What are you laughing at?" I snapped at Bob.

"It's funny."

"What's funny?"

"I dunno. She's laughing, so something's gotta be funny right!"

"Perhaps you're just got lucky with the case Mr Todd?" She had not reacted to my sharp insight as I expected.

"In what way?"

"Well, your sense of judgment is clearly way off."

"Always is," Bob chipped in. I so regretted allowing him to be in on this.

"Oh, I can assure you..."

"I'm not the client. Jenny is." Jenny and Vance had a one-night stand aeons ago pre-Victoria, resulting in a daughter. He gave Jenny a job and wanted to see them both right. Despite his philandering, drugs, fame, and the rest of it, she knew the inherent kindness of the man and knew it was no accident. It tore her apart when Lady Monaco and Vance split up. She had never liked Britney and thought her to be pure danger - calculating, determined, and lacking in any moral fortitude. Vance left a good trust fund to Mary and her daughter, which would look after them for the rest of their lives.

How did she find me? A friend of a friend of hers had been the client in one of my previous cases. That's how she had my email, business account details, and everything else.

"Why send me to Kitzbhuel to discover your partner in all this, Lady Monaco, did indeed skydive? That's what you wanted me to see right?"

"No, I wanted you to discover the love letters between Victoria and Vance. They were in the desk in the office. They would show she couldn't possibly have done such an act."

"I looked in there, but nothing." They all, including Bob, looked at me like a parent would look at a child with chocolate all over their face claiming they hadn't broken into the sweet jar. I regretted being slightly haphazard in my search.

"Sharp as a sausage," Bob said. I was starting to hate him.

"Why did you come to the pub the first time?" I asked Lady M.

"I was checking up on you. I love Jenny like a sister and didn't want her to blow her cash on a PI who didn't have a clue."

"He still doesn't," Bod added.

And so endeth the case of the dead rock star. My next one was a naked tech billionaire who'd been shot dead in a seedy motel room. It was totally out of my comfort zone, and it took Bob and me to the USA, a story in itself as he'd never been abroad before.

End
Thank you so much for reading this. The fact you've given your hard-earned cash, and the time out of your life to do so, fills me with deep gratitude and joy. If you enjoyed it, please do leave a rating or review here: http://www.amazhttp:// www.amazon.co.uk/review/create-review? &asin=B0BS48XRF6on.co.uk/review/create-review? &asin=B0B1QTNJSS

I've got loads of murders for Colin to solve and would love to know if you'd want to read them. I can also be easily found on socials with my ridiculously spelt first name.

So as the late great Dave Allen used to say, 'Goodnight, thank you, and may your God go with you.'

BOOKS BY THIS AUTHOR

Boo's Last Shot

An ex-pro battles his enemy on the course and betrayal off it, in this funny, light read.

Boomer (aka Boo), a world-famous Tour pro, retires having never won his dream prize - the Masters.

His best pal, Arlo, persuades him to come out of retirement and play in a new matchplay tournament. Boomer wants another shot at the big time and the ultimate goal of Augusta. This tourney is the first step to achieving his dream.

However, it's a fix organized by a psychotic gangster running a worldwide betting ring – and Arlo's in on it. Boomer's threatened with nasty violence if he doesn't play his part in the con.

He's forced to choose. Go against the gangster and face the consequences or beat his arch-enemy on the course. BUY NOW to find out which way he goes.

Rugby Club

A man who knows nothing about rugby has to save a club from going bust.

A shockingly awful team, with a coach who gave up on life long ago, enters a local tournament. They need to win it for the prize money that'll keep them from going bankrupt and closing down.

New owner, Ashley Havers, entered them into the tourney. He inherited Badcock RFC and despite being able to put his rugby knowledge on the back of a stamp, he's convinced he can take them all the way.

Just when it looks like it's all sorted, his world falls apart.

If Dodgeball (the film) met Ted Lasso (the series) on a rugby pitch, then this would be their lovechild.

BUY NOW to find out if he can rally the players and staff to save the club from impending demolition. A great light read.

Printed in Great Britain
by Amazon

43691089R00076